Julia James

THE GREEK'S MILLION-DOLLAR BABY BARGAIN

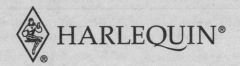

TORONTO • NEW YORK • LONDON
AMSTERDAM • PARIS • SYDNEY • HAMBURG
STOCKHOLM • ATHENS • TOKYO • MILAN • MADRID
PRAGUE • WARSAW • BUDAPEST • AUCKLAND

If you purchased this book without a cover you should be aware
that this book is stolen property. It was reported as "unsold and
destroyed" to the publisher, and neither the author nor the
publisher has received any payment for this "stripped book."

Recycling programs
for this product may
not exist in your area.

ISBN-13: 978-0-373-12805-1
ISBN-10:   0-373-12805-3

THE GREEK'S MILLION-DOLLAR BABY BARGAIN

First North American Publication 2009.

Copyright © 2009 by Julia James.

All rights reserved. Except for use in any review, the reproduction or
utilization of this work in whole or in part in any form by any electronic,
mechanical or other means, now known or hereafter invented, including
xerography, photocopying and recording, or in any information storage
or retrieval system, is forbidden without the written permission of the
publisher, Harlequin Enterprises Limited, 225 Duncan Mill Road,
Don Mills, Ontario, Canada M3B 3K9.

This is a work of fiction. Names, characters, places and incidents are
either the product of the author's imagination or are used fictitiously,
and any resemblance to actual persons, living or dead, business
establishments, events or locales is entirely coincidental.

This edition published by arrangement with Harlequin Books S.A.

® and TM are trademarks of the publisher. Trademarks indicated with
® are registered in the United States Patent and Trademark Office, the
Canadian Trade Marks Office and in other countries.

www.eHarlequin.com

Printed in U.S.A.

"You think a diamond necklace will get you into my bed."

She said it flatly, getting the words out past the emotion that was seizing on them as she spoke them.

"Why not? Your track record shows you are very amenable to such an approach to life." There was a twist to his mouth as he answered her, his voice terse.

It made the emotion spear deeper into her. Her eyes went to the necklace again—the necklace Nikos was offering her in exchange for sex. Emotion bit again—a different one. One that seemed to touch the very quick of her. But she must not allow *that* emotion, only the other one, which was as sharp as the point of a spear.

Her eyes pulled away, back to the man sitting in his handmade suit at his antique desk, rich and powerful and arrogant. A man who had kissed her deeply, caressed the intimacies of her body, who had melded his body with hers, who had transported her to an ecstasy she had never known existed.

Who was offering her a diamond necklace for sex....

Carefully, very carefully, she snapped shut the lid of the box and placed it back in front of him. "I am not," she said, "your mistress."

Dear Reader,

Harlequin Presents® is all about passion, power and seduction—along with oodles of wealth and abundant glamour. This is the series of the rich and the superrich. Private jets, luxury cars, international settings that range from the wildly exotic to the bright lights of the big city! We want to whisk you away every month to the far corners of the globe and allow you to escape to and indulge in a unique world of unforgettable men and passionate romances. There is only one Harlequin Presents®. And we promise you the world....

As if this weren't enough, there's more! More of what you love every month. Two weeks after the Presents® titles hit the shelves, four Presents® EXTRA titles go on sale! Presents® EXTRA is selected especially for you—your favorite authors and much-loved themes have been handpicked to create exclusive collections for your reading pleasure. Now there are more excuses to indulge! Each month there's a new collection to treasure—you won't want to miss out.

Harlequin Presents®—still the original and the best!

Best wishes,

The Editors

All about the author…
Julia James

JULIA JAMES lives in England with her family. Harlequin novels were the first "grown-up" books Julia read as a teenager, alongside Georgette Heyer and Daphne du Maurier, and she's been reading them ever since.

Julia adores the English and Celtic countrysides in all their seasons, and is fascinated by all things historical, from castles to cottages. She also has a special love for the Mediterranean—"The most perfect landscape after England!"—and considers both ideal settings for romance stories! Since becoming a romance writer, she has, she says, had the great good fortune to start discovering the Caribbean as well, and is happy to report that those magical, beautiful islands are also ideal settings for romance stories! "One of the best things about writing romance is that it gives you a great excuse to take holidays in fabulous places!" says Julia. "All in the name of research, of course!"

Her first stab at novel writing was Regency romances. "But alas, no one wanted to publish them!" she says. She put her writing aside until her family commitments were clear, and then renewed her love affair with contemporary romances. "My writing partner and I made a pact not to give up until we were published—and we both succeeded! Natasha Oakley writes for the Harlequin Romance line, and we faithfully read each other's works in progress and give each other a lot of free advice and encouragement!"

When she's not writing, Julia enjoys walking, gardening, needlework, baking "extremely gooey chocolate cakes" and trying to stay fit!

PROLOGUE

THE EXECUTIVE JET cut through the wintry night, heading north. Inside, its sole passenger stared through the darkened porthole. His face was sombre. His gaze unseeing. Looking inward, into the distant past.

Two boys, carefree, happy.

Brothers. Who'd thought they had all the time in the world.

But for one time had run out.

A knife stabbed into the heart of the man sitting, staring unseeing into the night sky beyond the speeding plane.

Andreas! My brother!

But Andreas was gone, never to return. Leaving behind only a weeping mother, a stricken brother.

And one precious, most miraculously precious gift of consolation…

The front doorbell rang, peremptory and insistent. Ann paused in clearing the mess in the kitchen and glanced into the second-hand pram, checking that the noise hadn't woken Ari. She hurried to the front door, pushing back untidy wisps of hair, wondering as she opened it who on earth it could be.

But even as she opened the door she knew who it was. He stood, tall, and dark, face set like stone. Beyond him, at the kerb, a chauffeured car, sleek and expensive, looked utterly out of place in this run down part of town.

'Miss Turner?'

The voice was deep, and accented. It was also cold, and very hard.

Ann nodded briefly, dread suddenly pooling in her stomach.

'I am Nikos Theakis,' he announced, as the breath caught in her throat in a shocked rasp. 'I have come for the child.'

Nikos Theakis. The man she had most cause to hate in all the world.

Ann could only stare, frozen, as he stepped past her, inside, dominating the narrow hallway, glancing dismissively around the shabby interior before arrowing back on her, as she stood shocked into immobility. 'Where is he?' he demanded.

His eyes lasered into her—dark, overpowering. Her mind was reeling. Out of all the insane things to do at this moment all she could do was stare at him. Stare at six foot of lean packed male, sheathed in a business suit that shouted wealth, sable hair immaculately cut, and a face—Ann's stomach clenched—a face that widened her eyes involuntarily.

Night-dark eyes, a strong blade of a nose, high cheek-bones, steel-jaw and sculpted, sensual mouth.

She gulped mentally. Then, with a jolt of effort, she dragged her mind away. What the hell was she doing, staring at the man like that? As if he were anyone other than the man he had just announced himself to be.

Nikos Theakis—rich, powerful, arrogant and ruthless. The man who had ruined her sister's life.

Because he had. Ann knew. Her sister had told her time and again.

Carla, always the golden girl, vibrant and glamorous. Partying her way through life. Then the party had ended. She'd turned up late last summer at Ann's poky, dingy flat with no place else to go. Distraught.

'He said he was crazy about me. Crazy! But now I'm pregnant and he won't marry me! And I know why.' Her beautiful face had twisted in hatred. 'It's that snobby bully-boy brother of his! The almighty Nikos Theakis. Looking down his nose at me like I'm dirt!'

Shocked, Ann had listened while Carla's tearful tirade flowed on. She had tried to reassure her, to remind her that the father of her child had to support it financially—

'I want Andreas to *marry* me!' Carla had railed.

The months that had followed had not been easy. Carla had sunk into a depressive lethargy, forbidding Ann to make contact with the father of her child even to at least sort out maintenance for the baby.

'Andreas knows where I am,' she'd said dully. 'I want him to come and find me! I want him to come and marry me!'

But Andreas had not come, and Carla's difficult pregnancy had ended with an even more difficult labour that had left her with postnatal depression, brought on, Ann was sure, by Andreas' rejection of her. To Ann had fallen the task of looking after baby Ari—for Carla, it seemed, had failed to bond, sinking deeper into depression, refusing all treatment.

The cure, when it had come, had been dramatic. A knock at the door—a young man, handsome, but with a strained, uncertain manner.

'I—I am Andreas Theakis,' he'd told Ann.

That was all it had taken. Carla had flown to him, her face transfigured. Her life transfigured. Or so she had believed. In reality it had been a little less romantic than Ann had hoped. Andreas had wanted a paternity test done.

'I have to convince my brother...' he'd said uneasily to Ann. But Carla had been viciously triumphant.

'Oh, Ari is Andreas', all right! And Mr Almighty Nikos Theakis is going to get his comeuppance! Andreas will marry me now—he's promised me, because he wants his son—and there isn't a thing his damn brother can do about it!'

Had Carla been tempting fate, to be so triumphant? Ann wondered, with a bitter twist of misery. It had not taken the malign will of Nikos Theakis to keep his brother from marrying her sister. It had taken a moment's misjudgement by Andreas, whisking Carla away—glamorous once more, vibrant once more—in his powerful hire car on unfamiliar British roads. Nothing more than that.

And two lives snuffed out.

Ann had been at home with Ari, looking after him willingly while Andreas and Carla went off for the day together. He had been orphaned at a stroke.

Ann knew that the horror and grief of that day would never leave her. Andreas's body had been flown back to Greece. None of his family had come near Ann. Ann had been left to bury her sister on her own. Left to look after baby Ari, all alone in the world now, except for her. She had made no attempt to contact Andreas' family. They had clearly never wanted Carla—never wanted her child. Whereas she…

Ari was all the world to her. All she had left. Her one consolation in a sea of grief. Grief for her sister and for the man she had so desperately wanted to marry. Anger for his brother—who had stopped them doing so. The brother who was now standing in her own hallway, eyes like lasers.

Demanding to take Ari from her.

Getting no answer, Nikos glanced into the empty room beside the front door, then strode down the narrow hallway to the kitchen at the end. His expression hardened even more. The place was a mess. There was a sink full of washing up, a plastic covered table with food debris on it. But it was the pram that drew him. He strode up to it and looked down. Emotion knifed through him. Andreas' son! Out of this nightmare, one shining miracle. He gazed down at the sleeping baby, his heart full. Slowly, he reached a hand towards him.

'Don't touch him!' The shrill whisper made him halt, whipping his head round.

Ann Turner was in the kitchen doorway, one hand closed tightly around the jamb. Nikos's brows snapped together. Did the girl think he was going to take the boy there and then? Obviously he was not. He would return when he had all the papers drawn up, a suitable nanny engaged, and then make an orderly removal of his nephew. He was here now simply because he had had to come. He had had to see for himself, this baby who was the only consolation in the nightmare that had closed over the Theakis family with Andreas's death.

His eyes rested a moment on the figure in the doorway, his mouth tightening as his gaze flicked over her. She suited the place. Shabbily dressed, with her hair tied back, an unkempt mess, and baby food on her shapeless T-shirt. She couldn't have looked less like the girl who had got her avaricious claws into his brother. Carla Turner had been a gilded bird of paradise. This sister of hers was a scrawny street sparrow.

But Ann Turner's appearance was irrelevant—only the baby in her care was important.

She was standing aside from the door now. 'Mr Theakis, I want you to leave. I've nothing to say to you, and I don't want you disturbing Ari.' Her voice was sharp. Hostile.

For a moment he said nothing, just went on looking at her. Ann could feel the colour run into her cheeks. The shock of seeing him was still jolting through her and she was fighting for composure. And losing. That soul-searching gaze of his was transfixing her. Then, without a word, he started towards her. She pulled aside swiftly as he brushed past her, striding down towards the front door. But her relief was short lived. He merely wheeled into the living room.

She hurried after him, heart thumping. 'Mr Theakis, I asked

you to leave—' she began, but he cut her short with a peremptory lift of his hand, as if she were a servant who had spoken out of turn.

'I am here merely to see the child for myself, and to inform you of the arrangements that have been made to take him home.'

Ann stared. 'This *is* his home.'

Nikos Theakis glanced around him. The sagging sofa, the worn carpet and faded curtains were encompassed in his condemning glance. 'This, Miss Turner,' he said, his eyes coming back to her, resting on her as if she were a cockroach, 'is not a home. It is a slum.'

Ann coloured. Poverty wasn't a crime! But Nikos Theakis clearly thought otherwise. His eyes were pinning her as if she were on a dissecting board. Instantly she became conscious of her messy, drab appearance and unwashed hair—conscious, inexplicably, of a feminine shame that she should be caught looking so absolutely unappealing in front of a man as expensively and physically drop-dead gorgeous as Nikos Theakis. Angrily, she broke her gaze away. What did it matter what she looked like? Or him? This was a man who'd just announced to her his intention of stealing the baby she loved more than anyone in the whole world. Her only living family.

Then suddenly he was speaking again, and this time his tone was quite different from the curt, condemning one with which he'd informed her she was living in a slum.

'But how could it be otherwise?' he said smoothly, as Ann's eyes flew to him again. 'It is very hard, is it not, Miss Turner, to have the unwelcome burden of a small baby? What girl your age could want that?'

His smooth words backfired. Instinctive rage reared in Ann. Yes, it was hard work looking after a baby. But Ari was never a burden. Never.

Nikos Theakis was speaking again, in the same smooth voice. 'So I shall relieve you of this unwanted burden, Miss

Turner, and you may return again to the life of a young, idle and carefree girl.'

She stifled down the rage that his unctuous words aroused in her, trying to keep her voice steady.

'Mr Theakis, you rejected Ari's existence from the moment he was conceived,' she shot at him witheringly. 'Why the sudden concern about him now?'

Nikos's eyes darkened. 'Because now I have the DNA results forwarded to me from the laboratory. I know that he is indeed my brother's son.' There was no trace of smoothness in his accented voice now.

'My sister said so right from the beginning!' Ann protested.

The sculpted mouth curled contemptuously. 'You think I would trust the word of a whore?'

It was spoken in such a casual way Ann blanched. 'Don't speak of Carla like that!' she spat furiously.

His eyes skewered her. 'Your sister slept with any man rich enough to keep her in the lifestyle she hawked herself out for. Of course I warned my brother to check the child was his.'

'My sister is *dead!*' she rang back at him.

'As is my brother. Thanks to her.' The coldness in his voice was Arctic. 'And now only one person is important—my nephew.' Abruptly his manner changed again. That surface smoothness was back in his voice. 'Which is why he must return to Greece with me. To have the life that his father would have wanted. Surely, Miss Turner, you cannot disagree with that?'

He sounded so smooth, so reasonable—but Ann's hackles did not go down. 'Of course I disagree! Do you propose, Mr Theakis—' she was even more withering now '—to raise Ari yourself? Or will you just dump him on a nanny?'

The dark eyes flashed. Ann felt a stab of angry satisfaction go through her. *He doesn't like being challenged!*

'To assuage your concerns, Miss Turner—' the deep voice

was inflected with sardonic bite '—Ari will live in the family home. Yes, with a professional nanny but, most crucially, with my mother.' And suddenly his voice that was quite different from anything Ann had heard so far. 'Do I really need to tell you how desperate my mother is for the only consolation she has left to her after the death of her son? Her grief, Miss Turner, is terrible.'

Involuntarily, Ann felt her throat tighten.

'She is welcome to visit any time she wants—' she began, but Nikos Theakis cut right across her.

'Generous of you, indeed, Miss Turner. But let us cut to the chase,' he said bitingly, the Arctic chill back in his voice.

His eyes were pinning her again, but this time there was not disdain in them for her shabby, messy appearance. Now they held the same expression as when he had called her sister a whore...

His voice was harsh as he continued. 'I expected no less of you, and you have ensured that my expectations are fulfilled. So, tell me—what price do you set on the boy's head? I know you must have a high one—your sister's was marriage to my brother. Yours, however, can only be cash. Well, cash it will be.'

Ann stared disbelievingly as Nikos Theakis slid a long-fingered hand inside his immaculately tailored jacket and drew out a leather-bound chequebook and a gold fountain pen. Swiftly, with an incisive hand, he scrawled across a cheque, then placed it on the table. His face was unreadable as her gaze flickered to it. Ann stood in shock as he spoke again. 'I never haggle for what I want, Miss Turner,' he informed her harshly. 'This is my first and final offer. You will get not a penny more from me. I am offering you a million pounds for my nephew. Take it or leave it.'

Ann blinked. This wasn't real. That piece of paper on the table in front of her wasn't a cheque for a million pounds—

a million pounds to buy a child. As she still stared, Nikos Theakis spoke again.

'My nephew,' he said, and once more he had resumed that smooth tone of voice, 'will have an idyllic childhood. My mother is a very loving woman, and will embrace her grandson into her heart. He will live with her in her home in Greece, at the Theakis villa on my private island, wanting for nothing.' He gave a small chilly smile. 'So, you see, you may take the money, Miss Turner, with a clear conscience.'

Ann heard his terrible words but they didn't register. Nothing registered except that piece of paper on the table in front of her. He saw her fixation upon it and his expression tightened. The deep lines around his mouth were etched more harshly. She kept on staring at the cheque.

Monstrous! *Monstrous!* Emotion swirled inside her and she felt the pressure build up in her chest as though it would explode. Only when he moved to the door could she tear her eyes away.

'I will leave you for now, and return at the end of the week,' he announced. 'All the paperwork will be completed by then, and you will hand my nephew over to me.' His voice hardened again. 'Understand that a condition of your payment is that all connection with my nephew is severed—he will not benefit from any communication with his late mother's relatives. However, since my mother can have no idea of the sordid life your sister led, or your squalid circumstances, she has asked me to give you this letter from her.' He slid his hand inside his jacket once more, and withdrew a sealed envelope, placing it beside the cheque. 'Do not think to reply to it. And do not attempt to cash your cheque yet—it is post-dated until I have my nephew.'

Then he was gone, closing the door behind him. Numbly Ann heard his footsteps on the pathway, then the soft clunk of a car door and the hushed note of an engine.

Her eyes went back to the cheque, disbelief and loathing

filling her. Then slowly her eyes went to the letter. Numbly she picked it up and opened it. Her heart was wrung as she began to read Sophia Theakis' words.

You cannot imagine, my joy when Nikos told me of Andreas' son. I felt the mercy of God's grace upon me. To be blessed with making a loving home for this tragically bereaved infant would be a privilege I pray for. If you can see it in your heart, despite your own grief for your lost sister, to grant me this prayer, and allow me to lay the love I had for my own son before his son, you will have my eternal gratitude. He will be cherished and loved throughout his life.

Forgive, I beg you, the selfishness of a woman who has lost her son, and for whom old age beckons, in desiring her grandchild to raise. But you are young and have your whole life before you, and you must be free to live it without assuming the premature responsibilities of motherhood to your sister's child which will consume your precious youth...

Ann could taste the terrible mix of grief and hope in every sentence. Her heart constricted. What should she do? What was for the best? Did Ari really have a ready-made, loving home waiting for him with his grandmother? Would it be better for him than the home she provided, or only richer? A child needed love—emotional security, above all. Far more than material security.

Ann's face shadowed with memory. Carla had been her emotional security as a child—all that Ann had had—and she had clung to her sister as the only constant in an uncertain, unstable world after their mother's death. Andreas' mother's words echoed in her head, offering 'a loving home for this tragically bereaved infant'. Was that what would be best for her nephew? Was it what Ari's parents would have wanted for their son? Ann's heart squeezed. She knew the answer already.

Andreas *would* have wanted his son raised in his family, by his own mother who had so clearly loved him. In the short time that she had known Andreas he had often mentioned his mother, with love and affection clear in his voice. His mother, he had told Ann, would welcome the news of Carla's existence—and their child she would welcome with open arms and open heart.

And Carla? What would she have wanted? Ann knew the answer to that question too, and a hand clutched her own heart. Carla had spent her brief life trying to claw her way to the wealth she thought meant happiness—she would have given her right arm for her son to take his place in the heart of the Theakis clan.

She had given more. She had given her life.

How can I keep Carla's son away from what she would have wanted so much for him? How can I?

Slowly, inexorable logic crushed her desperation to find reasons to keep the baby she loved so much. How could she? It would be pure selfishness on her part. If a loving, financially secure home were being offered to Ari, which both his parents would have wanted for him, how could she keep him within her own impecunious protection? However much she loved Ari, one day he would grow up. How would he feel then, having been deprived of the birthright that should have been his? The time to decide was now, while he was a baby— before emotional ties could be formed, before he grew to love her, and could be wounded by parting with her. Now was the time, she knew, for her to be strong—to let him go to his grandmother, to be cherished and loved, protected and safe.

As every child should be.

And there was yet one more reason for giving Ari up to his grandmother. One that she could not ignore. One that the monstrous offer by Nikos Theakis made it impossible to ignore.

A million pounds. *So much money.* How could she possibly say no to that?

Nikos stood, as he had stood only a few days before, in the dingy living room of Ann Turner's flat, watching with rigid features as she signed away her custody rights to his nephew. But as she put her name to the last of the legal papers, and shakily got to her feet, he allowed himself the satisfaction of letting his opinion of her show in his face.

Ann flinched. It was quite visible. Then his lawyer was picking up the papers and placing them inside his briefcase. At the door, a young nanny held Ari. For a second the emotion was so overpoweringly strong that she swayed with the need to snatch him back. Never, never let him go! But it was too late. The nanny, with a last sympathetic smile at Ann, was going, followed by the lawyer.

At the doorway, Nikos paused. Ann Turner was clutching the back of the chair, her face white. For a second Nikos frowned, then his face cleared, resuming its expression.

'You may cash your cheque now, Miss Turner,' he said softly, and his words licked over her like a whip.

But Ann was beyond his scorn. Beyond anything but the silent scream in her head that she could not do what she had just done. Yet even as the scream sounded in her mind Nikos Theakis was walking out, the front door closing behind him.

Its echo haunted her, tearing at her through the years ahead.

CHAPTER ONE

Four years later...

THE FAMOUS LONDON toy shop was crowded with children and parents as Ann threaded her way through, studying the myriad toys on offer. Most were far too expensive, but some gave her excellent ideas. It was strange being back in England. She'd hardly been back here at all in the years since she'd taken Nikos Theakis' cheque—and given Ari away.

Four years—and still guilt assailed her over what she had done. *Oh, Carla, did I do the right thing? Tell me I did. Tell me that Ari is loved and happy.*

That was all that mattered—that he was growing up, as Nikos Theakis had said he would, in an idyllic childhood: Orphaned, yes, but with family to love him and material wealth in abundance. Not all children were so fortunate.

She steeled herself. Yes, that was what she had to remember. Yet it was with a heavy sigh that she continued her perambulation. Being back in England brought back all the memories of Ari as a baby. Would she even recognise him if she saw him now? Her heart ached. Of all the strictures that Nikos Theakis had laid upon her, the loss of contact had been the worst to bear. But it was the price she'd had to pay.

Familiar blackness filled her as she thought of the man who

had taken Ari from her. Remembered the vile things he'd said about Carla, the contempt in his eyes when she'd taken his cheque. His banning her from ever seeing Ari again.

Eyes shadowed, she rounded a display of soft toys, pausing to check the price and flinching when she saw it. Then, across the aisle, she heard a voice that stilled her utterly.

'Ari, my darling, speak English—remember we are in England now.'

As if in slow motion, Ann's head turned. A little way away was a huge railway track, laid out with trains whizzing around. Children crowded to see it. Right in her line of sight was a small child, flanked by two women with their backs to Ann.

'That's the train Uncle Nikki is buying me!' came a piping voice.

The younger woman beside him turned to smile. Ann saw her profile and gasped, her hand flying to her throat. Four years might have passed, but Ann recognised instantly the nanny who had taken Ari from her arms. The little boy beside her must be…must be…

She felt faint with shock, staring, transfixed. Even as emotion convulsed her, the nanny's gaze shifted outwards slightly and caught hers. Ann could see her expression change as she recognised her. Then the older woman saw the nanny's expression, and turned as well.

It was Ari's grandmother. It had to be! For a moment the older woman, elegantly beautiful, but with a frail air about her, returned Ann's stare with mild curiosity, and then her brow puckered questioningly. She murmured something to the nanny, who nodded slowly, assessingly, then walked across to Ann.

'You will excuse me, please,' she said in an accented voice, curious and a little hesitant, 'but…is it possible…? Could you possibly be…? You have a look about you of my grand-son.'

Ann swallowed, unable to move, her throat still tight as a

leash. Then, into her eyeline came another figure. Much taller, male, clad in a black cashmere overcoat, striding towards the train display from the cash desk. Ann's breath caught in her throat. Simultaneously the man's head skewed round, his eyes searching for his mother, absent from his nephew, who was still absorbed in watching the trains scurrying round the track. They lighted on Ann and he stopped dead.

In a second she made her decision. She took half a step forward.

'Yes, I am Ann Turner. Ari's aunt,' she announced.

After that it became a blur. The expression on Sophia Theakis' face turned to pleasure, and she reached out her hands to take Ann's and draw her forward. Immediately Nikos Theakis strode up, his face like thunder. But his attempt to intercept the greeting was too late.

Sophia Theakis held up one small but imperious hand to her son. 'Nikki, this is quite extraordinary,' she said, speaking English. 'Look, this is little Ari's aunt. I can scarcely believe it!'

Her son's face might have been carved from stone. 'Extraordinary indeed,' he drawled, and the menace in his voice vibrated like a warning.

But Sophia Theakis did not hear it. Instead, she was drawing Ann towards where her grandson was still riveted by the train display. She laid a gentle arm on his shoulder, spoke something low in Greek and turned him around. For the first time in four long years Ann looked into the face of the little boy she had last seen as a tiny baby.

His face blurred as her eyes hazed with tears. She dropped down to a crouch and took his little hands.

'Hello, Ari,' she said quietly.

The child frowned slightly. 'Ya-ya says you are my *thia*. But I haven't got a *thia*, only a *thios*—Uncle Nikki. Are you married to Uncle Nikki? *Then* you would be my *thia*,' he reasoned, with impeccable logic.

Ann shook her head slightly. His grandmother said something, again in Greek.

'But I haven't got a mummy any more. She and my Daddy live in heaven,' said the little boy.

'Your mummy had a sister, Ari,' said Ann, her voice husky as she spoke. 'That sister is me.'

'Where have you been?' demanded Ari. 'Why have you not been to see me?' He sounded indignant as well as confused.

'I live very far away, Ari,' said Ann, trying to give the child an explanation he could cope with.

'Ari.' Nikos Theakis' deep voice cut curtly across hers. 'We are keeping Ya-ya waiting and delaying your…aunt. She is a very busy woman. I will accompany her to her taxi.'

His voice was as grim as his face, and as he spoke Ann felt his hand clamp heavily around her forearm. Removing her from the scene of her crime was evidently his first concern. But he had reckoned without treachery from within.

'Nikos!' said his mother, surprise and disapproval in her soft voice. She spoke to him rapidly in Greek, with the expressive use of her hands. As she spoke Ann saw his face harden, grow even grimmer. He bit something back to her, and shot a glowering glance in Ann's direction. His mother raised astonished eyebrows, then said something again in Greek to her son.

Nikos Theakis' face set, then he gave a brief, curt nod. 'As you wish,' he said tightly, in English.

Sophia Theakis smiled, and then turned that smile on Ann. Graciously, she invited Ann to lunch, taking Ann's hands in hers.

'I have longed to meet you for many years, my dear child,' she said in her warm voice. She tucked Ann's hand in her arm. 'Come,' she said.

Ann was in a daze, scarcely able to believe what was happening. They left the store and were conveyed by chauffeured car

to the hotel where the Theakis party were evidently staying—
one of London's premier hotels, overlooking Green Park.

Ann only had eyes for Ari who, realising he had a brand-
new admirer, took full advantage, chattering away to her. Yet,
despite her undivided attention to the little boy, Ann could not
help but feel the dark, glowering presence of his uncle, his
anger at her vibrating from every pore, condemning her for
her temerity in daring to be there. She ignored it. What did
she care if Nikos Theakis were wishing her to oblivion? She
returned the compliment tenfold!

Her only concern was Ari.

Her heart clenched again as she took in the miraculous
reality of seeing her nephew here, now, in the flesh—a little
boy, no longer a baby, no longer only a wrenching memory....

Lunch passed in a daze as well. What she ate she had no
idea. She had no idea of anything except the fact she was sitting
at a table with Ari, asking him all the questions a child his age
would be ready to answer—his favourite toys and stories and
activities. He regaled her copiously, prompted sometimes by
his nanny, Tina, and sometimes by his grandmother.

His uncle, however, spoke only when referred to by his
nephew. This, however, was not seldom, and Ann could see
that Nikos Theakis was regarded as a high authority and the
fount of great wisdom by his nephew. What she also had to
accept—and she knew she should be glad of it—was how
patient and attentive he was to Ari, and how Ari showed no
timidity or reticence with him. As for his grandmother—it was
obvious to Ann that Ari was the apple of her eye.

Across the years, the ghost of her voice, so heartrending
in the letter she had written for Ann, echoed in her head: *He
will be cherished and loved throughout his life.*

Oh, Carla, thought Ann, her throat catching with emotion.
You can be happy—you can be happy at how safe and loved
your son is!

A small beringed hand was laid lightly on her wrist. It was Ari's grandmother. 'You are thinking of your sister?' she said, her eyes kind.

Ann could only nod, unable to speak. The older woman smiled sadly.

'We do not know why they were taken from us—your sister and my dear son—but we know they gave us a gift beyond price. And I am so pleased—*so* pleased, my dear—that you are here with us now, after far, far too long away from Ari.'

Again, Ann could not speak—but this time not because of the emotion of grief. What could she say to this kind, sympathetic woman of how cruel the separation had been for her? How cruel, too, her surviving son's strictures on Carla and herself.

She looked away—and straight into dark, hard eyes. Time buckled, and it was if she were once more standing in front of Nikos Theakis in her dingy flat, with him looking at her as if she were a cockroach. Almost she dropped her eyes under that killing basilisk gaze, but then she rallied, her chin lifting slightly, her eyes clashing with his. Then, as she continued to hold his gaze defiantly, refusing to back down, his expression began to change. She didn't know what it was, but something shifted in those hooded night-dark eyes, and as it shifted something quivered down the length of her spine…something that suddenly made her snap her gaze away after all.

Then Ari made some childishly amusing remark, causing her to smile, as well as his grandmother and nanny, and the moment was gone.

As the meal came to an end, Sophia Theakis took Ann's hands again, drawing her to her feet.

'For the moment, alas, we must say goodbye again, while I place myself in the hands of my doctors.' She spoke lightly, but Ann wondered what it was that had brought her to London for medical treatment. Then Ari's grandmother was speaking again. 'But this must not be the end of our acquaintance.

Within a week I shall be returning to Greece for our Easter celebrations, and then, dear child, if it is at all possible, I shall count it the greatest pleasure if you will be my guest there. On Sospiris you shall finally have a chance to make up for the years you have lost with little Ari.' She smiled benignly.

'My son will make all the arrangements. Nikos—' She spoke swiftly in Greek, clearly giving him some kind of instruction. He nodded curtly at the end.

'I will indeed,' he said grimly. 'With the greatest pleasure, I will escort Miss Turner to her destination.'

Dark eyes rested on Ann, and she did not need to be a mind-reader to know where it was that Nikos Theakis wanted her destination to be. Somewhere exceedingly hot would do nicely. With flames.

Nikos closed his hand over the rich material of her coatsleeve, his grip tightening on the arm beneath. Tightly leashed anger lashed within him, as it had been doing since his incredulous gaze had first landed on the figure daring—*daring!*—to speak to his mother in the toy store.

Theos mou, he should have expected this! Should have expected that the girl would make such an attempt! Doubtless the million pounds he'd paid her off with had all been frittered away by now.

His brow darkened. Had it been deliberate? Positioning herself in that toy store, richly arrayed as she was in the spoils of her ill-gotten gains? Of course it had! Why was he even questioning it? What else would a girl like her have been doing in a toy store of all places? No, she must have plotted it deliberately, after discovering—he had yet to find out how!—that his mother was visiting London with Ari, and seeking the opportunity to put herself forward. More fool him for not having expected it. For letting her take him totally by surprise…

In more ways than one. For a moment Nikos felt again the second of the two shocks that had hit him as he'd recognised the woman accosting his mother. Not the rage that had signalled the moment he registered that it was Ann. But the other one. The one that had almost made him look twice, as if his eyes were deceiving him. Deceiving him that the woman with the knockout face and figure could possibly be the same drab, unkempt girl he'd last seen four years ago.

But then, he thought cynically, it was amazing what a million pounds to spend on herself could achieve by way of improvement! Sleek, beautiful hair, subtle make-up, flattering designer clothes and—his cynicism deepened—an expensive winter tan on flawless skin. Oh, yes, Miss Ann Turner with a million pounds at her disposal could well afford never to be drab and repellent ever again! Now she could look every inch a man-trap, like her trollop of a sister...

Not that she was anything like as blatant as her sister. Carla Turner had flaunted the kind of sugar-babe looks that pulled men in the most obvious way possible—including his gullible brother!—but Ann Turner was in a quite different style.

Classy.

The word came to him, and irritated him even more. Yet the woman whose arm his own was now pinioning had fitted in as effortlessly with the hotel dining room and their party as if she had been born to it.

His eyes went to her rigid profile, and assessed it.

Yes, classy. Her *soigné* hairstyle, the discretion of her make-up and the restrained chic of her outfit all created that image.

But it was more than just classiness...

His eyes lingered, and he felt again, angering him, the same reaction he'd felt as his eyes had first settled on her. He knew what it was, that reaction—it was a familiar one to him, and one he usually enjoyed. But *not* when it came in response to a woman like the one he was frog-marching out of the hotel

and away from his family...who should never have been
allowed to contaminate it in the first place.

What the hell had his mother been thinking of? But even
as he posed the question he knew the answer. He'd deliberately sheltered her from the sexually sordid truth about
Andreas' disastrous involvement with Carla Turner, and the
financially sordid truth about her sister. So no wonder she had
taken Ann Turner at face value.

Anger bit in him again—he would have loved to expose
the girl for the worthless sham she was, but he would not upset
his mother. His brother's death had nearly destroyed her, and
Ari had become her only reason to keep going. With her
health still frail, he would never upset her by exposing the
truth about Ann Turner. But a free lunch was all the girl was
going to get. Nothing more.

He thrust her inside a taxi at the hotel entrance, and came
in after her. Immediately she slid to the farthest side of the
seat, away from him. Illogically, the move annoyed him. Who
did Ann Turner think she was to flinch away from him?

He ordered the taxi driver to 'just drive'. Then he turned
on his target.

Ann tried to keep the maximum distance from him, but Nikos
Theakis seemed to take up far too much space—exacerbated
by the way he'd thrown his arm along the back of the seat,
stretching out his long legs into the well of the cab.

Four years had made him even more formidable and grim-
faced—and his impact was just as overpowering. He was still
ludicrously good-looking, but now he looked tougher than
ever. He must be into his thirties now, she reckoned swiftly,
and the last remnants of youth were long gone. He looked
hard, arrogant, and as self-assured as ever. Wealth and power
radiated from him. A lot more radiated from him as well...

No! She crushed down the realisation. It was as inappro-

priate now as it had been four years ago. Worse than inappro-
priate—wrong. Wrong to pay the slightest attention to the fact
that Nikos Theakis had the kind of looks to turn female heads
for miles around. The *only* thing about Nikos Theakis she had
to register was that she hated him…

Hated him for despising Carla, hated him for taking Ari
from her, hated him for paying her to take him…

No—she wouldn't think about that either. It was gone, in
the past. And the money was spent, too. All gone now. So she
would not let him intimidate her now any more than he had
four years ago. She sat in her corner, back stiff, and met his
coruscating gaze unflinchingly. It seemed to make him angrier
yet. With a rasp in his deep voice he began his attack.

'Doubtless, Miss Turner, you think yourself very clever
indeed, insinuating yourself into my family thanks to my
mother's innocence and kind nature!' His dark eyes narrowed
viciously. 'But make no mistake. You will not be allowed to
capitalise on scraping an acquaintance with her. This,' he
assured her grimly, 'was your first and last meeting.'

Nikos Theakis' mouth tightened. Irrelevantly, Ann registered the sensual twist to it, and then he was continuing his
condemnation of her.

'You have no place in my nephew's life—*no place*—do
you understand? That was the agreement you made, was it
not, four years ago, when you sold your dead sister's baby to
me for cash?'

The scorn in his voice excoriated her. Ann felt herself
flushing beneath its venom. She opened her mouth to retali-
ate, but his eyes flicked over her like a whip.

'And I can see just where the cash went.' His hand, resting
along the back of the seat, dipped to touch the fleece of her
coat's shoulder, trailing one finger down her upper arm.
'Cashmere,' he murmured, his tone changing suddenly from
angry to smooth, his long lashes sweeping down over his

eyes. 'So soft. So warm.' His mouth twisted. 'So expensive. Tell me,' he went on in that dangerous voice, 'has the million pounds all gone? Is that why you have decided to break your agreement and try to stick your greedy little fingers into the Theakis honey pot once more?'

The hand was still on Ann's sleeve, idly brushing the soft fabric. It should have been a harmless gesture, but it wasn't. It should have been intangible through the layers of her coat and the sleeve of her dress beneath, but it wasn't. Ann felt that light touch all the way through to her skin. Felt it, out of nowhere, cut right through her anger and resentment to reach the quick...

Her heart started to beat more heavily and her eyes were dragged to his. They were very dark, the eyes of Nikos Theakis, half closed as they surveyed her all over, from the pale gleaming crown of her gilt-blonde head, sweeping on across the fine bones of her face, dwelling a moment on her long-lashed grey eyes, then on down the slender curves of her body to the long, shapely length of her stockinged legs.

The breath caught in her throat. It was that moment again— the one that had happened so fleetingly, so briefly, at the end of lunch—the one that she had deliberately ignored, refused to acknowledge. But now she could not ignore it...

Four years ago this man had consigned her to the realms of the sexually repulsive. He'd cast one look at her messy, drab appearance and dismissed her.

He wasn't dismissing her now.

The dark eyes washed over her leisurely, keeping the breath stifled in her lungs, the muscles of her throat constricted. Her heart was giving slow, ponderous slugs as everything seemed to slow down, inside and out. The traffic noise faded, everything faded except the pulse in the hollow of her neck, the tightness of her lungs. She tried to fight it, tried to draw breath—but she couldn't. Could only go on sitting there as his eyes came back to her—reading her reaction.

He smiled.

It was not a nice smile, but it made a pool of heat flush all the way through Ann's body. He watched the heat flood through her as if it were a visible wave, his dark eyes veiled as they looked over her, through her.

The air in the taxi was thick, tangible. She felt his hand lift from her shoulder and reach a little further. Then the pad of his index finger was touching her cheek, drawing down it like a knife blade. Her eyes were locked on his—she could not break away.

She shivered.

The hand dropped, and rested again innocuously on the back of the taxi seat. But it had done its damage. She felt his touch sear her cheek as if his hand were still there. As if his touch had burnt into her skin…

'I will tell you how it will be, Miss Turner,' Nikos Theakis informed her, as though he were having a normal conversation with her. His voice had become flat and unemotional. All trace of his awareness of her as a female had vanished, as if a light had been switched off. 'There will be no more Theakis money for you. You have had your pay off. If you have squandered it, that is your misfortune. You will have no opportunity to take advantage of my mother's generosity and sentimental kind-heartedness.' His voice flattened even more, and the dark eyes beheld her opaquely. 'Accordingly, there will be no little holiday for you on Sospiris. No continuation of this touching reunion with the child you sold for a million pounds so that you could buy yourself a worthless lifestyle for a few years. No further contact with my nephew or my family at all. Do you understand me?'

Ann bit her lip. She longed to yell back at him but what was the point? She already knew she could not accept Mrs Theakis's invitation—it was *impossible,* impossible. She did not need Nikos Theakis telling her that, ordering her to stay away from Ari.

Seeing Ari again like this, out of the blue, had been a miracle—a wonderful gift. But that was all it was. Oh, now that Mrs Theakis had met her perhaps Ann would finally be allowed to write to Ari, send him presents, even occasionally see him—but she could never be part of his life. She knew that—accepted that. Had long ago accepted that.

So all she said now was a tight lipped, 'Yes, I understand, Mr Theakis.'

'That is as well,' he said curtly, lifting his hand to rap on the cabby's glass. 'I see we understand each other. Make sure it stays that way, Miss Turner.'

Then the taxi was stopping, and Nikos Theakis was climbing out, having pressed a twenty-pound note into the cabby's hand and told him to take his remaining passenger wherever the fare warranted. Then, briefly, he turned his attention back to Ann.

'Stay away from my family.'

Then he strode off into the London crowd, and Ann could see him no more.

For the second time in four years Nikos Theakis had walked out of her life.

He would walk back in far more swiftly.

CHAPTER TWO

ANN HAD JUST returned to her flat with a bagful of groceries. She had heard nothing more from Ari's grandmother, though she had posted a polite thank-you letter to the hotel, thanking her for lunch and for her kindness in letting her have such precious time with Ari. It saddened her profoundly that she would never know him as she longed to, but at least she knew now that he was having the happiest of childhoods, with a doting grandmother and, she forced herself to acknowledge, an uncle who clearly held his nephew in affection, despite his harsh condemnation of his mother and aunt.

She gained the kitchen and started to unpack the groceries. The front doorbell rang. Frowning slightly, for she was not expecting anyone, Ann trotted down the narrow hallway and cautiously opened the door.

But not cautiously enough. Like an action replay from four years ago, Nikos Theakis strode inside.

'We,' he announced balefully to an open-mouthed Ann, 'shall speak.'

'You want me to do what?' she demanded, staring down at Nikos Theakis disbelievingly. He was sitting in the armchair by the window of the living room, and his expensive, bespoke tailored presence was as dominatingly incongruous as it had been four years ago.

'Spend a month in Greece, at my mother's house on Sospiris,' repeated the man who'd told her to stay away from his family.

'Why?' she asked bluntly, folding her arms defensively over her chest. She was wearing jeans today, and the top she was wearing with them suddenly seemed to be showing off her figure voluptuously. Nikos Theakis' gaze had swept over her as he'd walked in and sat himself down without a by-your-leave, and she had not liked it.

But then there was nothing about Nikos Theakis she liked. Least of all the way he was speaking to her now.

He was angry. That was obvious. It was suppressed anger, but anger all the same, leashed on a tight rein. It had not stopped him flicking his gaze over her in a way that had brought a flush to her cheek—a flush that had nothing to do with the fact that she not expected to set eyes on him again and did not want to anyway. Even if her insides *had* given a sudden gulp as she'd rested her eyes on him…on his tall, powerful frame…the hard, handsome face and those night dark eyes.

Then all other thoughts had vanished from her head as he had dropped his bombshell.

'You are to come to Sospiris because,' he bit out, 'my mother insists! And,' he ground out even more bitingly, 'as her doctor informs me that her heart condition will be exacerbated by any emotional upset, I have no option but to concede to her wishes. Well?' he demanded, tight lipped. 'What are you waiting for? Start packing.'

Ann crushed her arms more tightly over her chest.

As if in an action replay from four years ago, Ann watched him reach into his suit jacket, take out his leather-bound chequebook, hook one leg over his knee to create a writing platform, and fill out a cheque with his gold fountain pen. He presented it to her with a contemptuous flourish.

'The fee, Miss Turner, for your very expensive and valuable time.'

His opinion of her cut through his voice.

Numbly she took the piece of paper he proffered her. The zeros blurred, then resolved themselves. She gave a faint sigh of shock and her eyes widened.

'Ten thousand pounds, Miss Turner.' Nikos Theakis' hatefully sarcastic voice floated over her head somewhere. 'Now, that is what I call an expenses-paid holiday…'

Slowly, Ann shifted her gaze so that she met his eyes. The expression in them could have incinerated her on the spot. Answering emotion seared her breast. With one part of her she wanted to rip the cheque into a dozen pieces and throw them in his cold, contemptuous face. And with another she felt a gush of excited anticipation at seeing her nephew again, combined with the sudden rush of realisation that she held ten thousand pounds in her hands. A fortune—and one that she knew exactly how to spend.

Just the way she had spent her last cheque from Nikos Theakis.

A smile of sweet pleasure broke across her face. 'Why, Mr Theakis,' she said saccharinely, knowing just how angry she could make him, and how satisfying that would be to her insulted soul, 'how very, very generous of you. I believe I shall start packing straight away.'

As she turned away, heading for the stairs, a word slithered out of the sculpted, sensual mouth. She couldn't tell what it was, because it was Greek. But it was enunciated with such deadly venom that she did not request a translation.

For a moment Ann stood transfixed, as if he'd struck her physically, not just verbally. Then, back stiffening, she gave a tiny, indifferent shrug of her shoulders and walked out of the room to begin her packing.

* * *

Ann craned her neck as the helicopter swooped in to land on the helipad behind the Theakis villa. Set in a huge, landscaped Mediterranean garden, on the tiny private island of Sospiris, the villa was breathtakingly beautiful—gleaming white, its walls and terraces splashed with bougainvillea, the vivid hues of an azure swimming pool competing with the even more azure hues of the Aegean all around. As they disembarked, she gazed around her, revelling not just in the beauty of the surroundings, but in the balmy warmth after the chill British spring.

Nikos Theakis watched her reaction as she stared about her, visibly delighted. 'Worth getting your greedy little claws into, Miss Turner?' he murmured.

Ann ignored him, as she had done her best to do all the way from London on the private jet that had flown them to the Greek mainland. He had returned the favour, occupying himself with his laptop and a pile of what she had assumed were business documents.

But if Nikos Theakis made it crystal clear she was here very nearly over his dead body, the warmth of his mother's greeting almost equalled the exuberance of her grandson's, who had swooped on his newly discovered aunt with a fierce hug from so little a body. As she crouched down to return his embrace, Ann's eyes misted.

Oh, Carla—if you could see your son now. How happy he is, how much he is part of the family you wanted for him. And this would have been Carla's home too—she would have been bringing her son up here, in this beautiful villa, married to Andreas, in the perfect life that her sister had so longed for. Instead a grave had been waiting for her, and for the man she'd so wanted to marry…

Anguish crushed Ann, then resolutely she put it aside. The past was gone—it could not be undone. Only the present was left, and the future that was Carla's and Andreas' son.

* * *

Nikos watched Ann Turner entering the salon that one of the house staff was ushering her into. He had seen nothing of her since he had handed her over to his mother on their arrival at the villa that afternoon, taking refuge from his grim mood by incarcerating himself in his study. Work, at least, had taken his mind off the unwelcome presence of a woman he wished to perdition, but who had, instead, succeeded in further insinuating himself into his family. Now, however, he was face to face with her again. His gaze surveyed her impassively. But impassiveness was not the hallmark of his mood. Resentment and grim anger were. And another thing he resented, even more than her presence.

Her impact on him as a woman.

His mouth tightened as he watched her approach his mother. Damn the girl—why did she have to look like that? Why couldn't she still look the way she had four years ago? Why did she have to be wand slender, with that incredible hair swept back off her face, her classically beautiful features set off by an aqua knee-length dress in some fine jersey material that skimmed her lissom body, making her look both subtly alluring and yet not obviously so. Why did he have to wonder what it might be like to sift his fingers through that long hair, inconveniently restrained in a velvet tie? Why did he have to speculate whether her breasts, scarcely outlined in the discreetly styled dress, would repay his personal investigation?

Forcibly, he dragged his eyes away from her towards his mother. She was smiling graciously at her guest, holding out a hand to invite her to join her on the sofa for pre-dinner drinks. Nikos felt his mood worsen. Watching his mother smile, bestow her kindness, her favour, on so worthless an object, galled him bitterly—yet there was nothing he could do about it. Not without hurting his mother, shocking her with the squalid truth about Ari's aunt.

No, like it or not—and he did *not*—he would have to endure

this farce, and make sure it ended as swiftly as possible, with the least opportunity for Ann Turner to get her greedy little claws yet deeper into both his coffers and his family.

She was greeting his mother prettily now, in halting phrase-book Greek, which set Nikos' teeth on edge but drew a warm smile of approval from his mother. Then she was taking the place indicated to her, and smiling her thanks as one of the staff offered her a drink. Moodily, Nikos seized his martini from the manservant's tray. He felt in need of its strengthening powers tonight.

'So, my dear child,' his mother was saying to her guest, 'I hope you have had an enjoyable afternoon with little Ari? Was I wrong to let him monopolise you so much on your very arrival? But he has been so eager for you to come.'

Ann smiled warmly. 'I've had a wonderful time! He is such a lovely little boy, Kyria Theakis,' she said spontaneously. 'Thank you—thank you so much for all you have done for him...'

Her voice threatened to break, and she fell silent.

'My dear,' said Sophia Theakis, reaching out her small hand to touch Ann's. 'He is our own precious child, is he not? We love him for himself—and for the memory he brings of those we have loved and who are no more.'

As tears pricked in Ann's eyes she felt her hand squeezed briefly, comfortingly. She blinked, looking away—straight into a pair of hard, dark eyes. Nikos Theakis' scathing gaze as he beheld this affecting scene.

Her own gaze hardened in response. She would not let this obnoxious man judge her—condemn her. She turned away, back to Mrs Theakis.

'Now,' Ari's grandmother went on, 'you must allow me to introduce my dear cousin, Eupheme, who is so very kind as to keep me company and take charge of the beautiful garden we have here which she created for us all.'

Another woman of late middle-age—who had, Ann

realised, just entered by a different door on the other side of the room—came forward now. Ann stood up and waited as Mrs Theakis performed the introductions. Again, Ann murmured in phrasebook Greek. It drew a kind smile from her hostess's companion, and an answer in Greek, which was swiftly translated for her by Mrs Theakis, who added that Cousin Eupheme spoke little English.

The topic of the conversation returned to Ari, and Ann was more than happy for it to do so, turning away from Nikos Theakis. Yet she felt him watching her like a malevolent bird of prey. The back of her neck prickled.

Why did the damn man get to her like this? She didn't like him—he didn't like her. God knew he had made that clear enough! Well, she didn't care about that—didn't care anything about him—cared only that she was here, in Ari's home, for the first time in her life. She would not let Nikos Theakis spoil so treasured an occasion for her.

This was difficult, for Nikos Theakis in a white dinner jacket that set off his natural tan and his strong, ludicrously good-looking features, was hard to ignore, though Ann did her dogged best. Surely she couldn't care less that he was a darkly stunning specimen of the male species, compelling and magnetic—this man who had called her sister a whore? Her mouth tightened as she took her place at the beautifully burnished dining table indoors.

Nevertheless, thanks to Mrs Theakis' impeccable skills as an experienced hostess, dinner passed comfortably enough, helped by the fact that Nikos Theakis contributed little more than his glowering presence at the table.

'You have arrived at a time that is both happy and sad for us, my child,' her hostess remarked at one point. 'Perhaps Tina has already told you that she is to be married from this house shortly? Her fiancé, Dr Forbes, is an archaeologist, excavating on our larger neighbour, Maxos. Indeed, she is spending the evening with him there tonight. I am happy for her, of course, but I confess I shall miss her—and Ari even more so, for she has been an essential part of his family since he came here. So your arrival will serve to divert him from his impending loss.'

'I'd be delighted to divert him,' enthused Ann, and the conversation moved on again.

After dinner, they removed to the salon for coffee, but it was not long before Ann, feeling the strain of the day, opted to retire to bed. As if the punctilious host, Nikos escorted her to the door in a parody of politeness. Away from his mother and Eupheme, Ann could feel once more the assessing, leisurely flick of his eyes over her, lingering a moment on the swell of her breasts. To her flustered dismay, she felt them tightening beneath his scrutiny.

'Another beautiful garment—and one that flatters your beauty,' he murmured in a low voice. 'I am glad to see you disposed so tastefully of my money...'

His smile was like the baring of a jackal's teeth. She turned her head sharply away and strode off across the wide, marble-floored hallway towards the staircase, sure that she heard a soft, jibing laugh behind her.

Damn him, why did he get to her like that? Why should she care what Nikos Theakis thought of her? He was nothing to her—*nothing*.

I'm here for Ari—that's all.

That was what she must remember—only that.

Tina reinforced Ann's determination the next day. The two women were on the beach in front of the villa, watching Ari industriously dig a very large, deep hole in the sand some little way away. Tina, so similar to her in age, with a friendly personality, was easy company. She was full of praise for both Mrs Theakis and Nikos Theakis. The former Ann could well understand, but her expression must have showed her doubt about the latter.

'Nikos is a fantastic employer,' enthused Tina. 'Incredibly generous. He's sponsoring Sam's dig, you know, and letting me have my reception at the villa. Plus he's wonderful with Ari, and is devoted to his mother's welfare too.'

Yes, thought Ann, *enough to force himself to pay me a ridiculous amount of money to come here because she wants me here!*

Aloud, she simply murmured, 'I suppose that's understandable, given Mrs Theakis' frail health.'

Tina's eyes lit. 'Is it, though? You know, I suspect that Mrs Theakis finds her poor health very useful! Nikos was dead set against the trip to London, saying it would be too tiring for her, but lo and behold Mrs Theakis' doctor recommended a heart specialist there, so off we all went! Mind you,' she went on, 'he's nowhere near so co-operative with other women! As you can imagine, with his looks and money, women are all over him—and desperate to become Mrs Nikos Theakis. But he won't be caught by any of them! He just enjoys them, then it's over. But of course he gets away with it. Men like that do.' She shrugged good-humouredly, then turned her attention back to her charge. 'Ari, pet, how's that hole coming along? Can we come and see it yet?'

The rest of the morning was spent with Ari, but after lunch, while Ari had his afternoon nap, Ann could no longer resist the lure of the swimming pool. Sliding into its silky azure depths, she did a few taxing lengths, then slowed to a leisurely breaststroke. Her wet hair streamed behind her, sleeked off her face, and the sun glittered in her eyes, warming her with its rays, as she moved soothingly, rhythmically through the water. A sense of well-being filled her at the peace and quiet and beauty of it all.

Until, with the strangest prickling in the back of her neck, she started to feel uneasy. Reaching the far end of the pool, she halted, holding the marble edge and looking around her.

She saw him immediately. On an upper terrace, one hand resting on the balustrade, looking down at her.

Nikos Theakis.

Instantly she felt vulnerable—exposed. Instinct told her to get out of the water as fast as she could and grab a towel. But that would mean he'd see her, and out of the pool she'd be even more exposed than with the translucent veil of the water. For a moment she hesitated, then, with a splash, she plunged back into the water, swimming again. After another two lengths she glanced surreptitiously up at the balcony again. To her relief, no one was there. Quickly, she got out of the pool and wrapped her towel around her tightly, recovering her composure.

She would not feel intimidated by Nikos Theakis! Recklessly, she settled down to sunbathe, lying on her tummy and loosening her bikini top to expose her back. As she lay soaking up the sun she started to feel drowsy in the quietness and warmth, and felt herself slipping away into sleep.

Dreams came, hazy and somnolent, drifting through her unconscious mind, scarcely registering.

Except one.

She felt in her dream a shadow falling over her, and then a hand stroking down the bare length of her sun-warm spine with a slow, caressing touch. She murmured something, nestling her face into the cushion. Then dreamless sleep closed over her once more.

Beside the lounger Nikos stood, watching her motionless form. His face was shuttered.

Why had he just done that? Why had he succumbed to the impulse he'd experienced when he'd taken a break from his work, gone out on to the terrace outside his office to get a breath of fresh air, and seen that lissom figure cutting smoothly through the water, the sunlight shimmering on her barely veiled body? He should have gone straight back indoors. Instead, he had gone on watching her, until she'd glanced up and caught him watching.

Abruptly, annoyed that she'd seen him looking at her, he'd gone back to his office. But he hadn't settled. And before ten minutes were up he'd pushed his chair back restlessly and gone out on the terrace again. She'd get out of the pool now, sunning herself.

His eyes had gone to her immediately. To the slender body, the sculpted perfection of her back, the narrow indent of her waist and the gentle swell of her hips, rounding down into long, gazelle legs.

He'd felt himself respond to the image, unable to look away, annoyed with himself for succumbing. Even more annoyed when he'd found he had started to walk down the flight of steps to the pool level, had strolled across to her, to see her in close-up, and worse, had succumbed to the impulse to lower a hand to her exposed nape, then glide it slowly, leisurely, down the elegant length of her spine.

She was like silk to touch...

He snapped his hand away.

Hell, this was not supposed to be happening. He shouldn't be responding to the damn girl! He was supposed to be ignoring her, being wise, totally wise, to the allure she held for him!

Because anything else was folly. Folly and madness. He knew exactly what Ann Turner was, and despite the beautiful packaging the woman inside was venal and worthless.

If she'd thrown that cheque back in his face—told him that no power on earth could part her from her nephew—then he might have thought better of her! But, no, she hadn't been able to take her eyes from the cheque...

For a long moment he simply stood, looking broodingly down on her sleeping, near naked form.

She really was lovely...so very tempting..

No. Cost him what it would, he must remember the only important thing about Ann Turner—she had sold her nephew to him for cash, and was here only because she was hoping for yet more money from the Theakis coffers. That was all he must keep in his mind.

Everything else was—irrelevant.

Abruptly, he turned away. There was work to be done. On swift, disciplined strides, he went back to his office, closing the doors to the terrace behind him with a decided snap.

Ann's sleep ended abruptly some time later when Ari, energy levels recharged from his nap, emerged with Tina, like a miniature rocket in swimming trunks and armbands. A hectic water playtime ensued, followed by refreshments at the edge of the pool, where they were joined by Ari's grandmother and Cousin Eupheme.

Sitting on a swing seat, Ari beside her, chattering away, Ann found herself thinking that although she had been here only such a short time, she fitted in as easily and naturally as if there had been no dark history keeping her away, parting her from Ari. But she knew exactly why she was feeling comfortably at ease now—because Nikos Theakis wasn't there, casting his malign, intimidating shadow over everything.

She had to face him again over dinner, however. She'd come up from the nursery quarters with Tina, who was not with her fiancé that evening, after helping her put Ari to bed. Once again she'd read him to sleep, and as she'd dropped one last light kiss on his forehead she'd felt a lump form in her throat.

Carla's son. Happy and secure.

Her memories swept back to the days of her own childhood, when her whole universe had been her older sister, to whom she had clung in the frightening, confused times they had both faced. In those fearful years where would she have been without Carla to hold her, to kiss her goodnight, to be all the family she had? And here, now, she was kissing Carla's son goodnight—who had no mother of his own.

But Ari's happy, she thought, fighting down the lump. *He does not miss the parents he never had. He has his grandmother, and his uncle, and a kind and affectionate nanny. And now, for this brief time, he has me.*

The briefness of her time with him clutched at her heart like a cold hand. Then anger stabbed in its stead. *Damn Nikos Theakis!* she thought. *Damn his arrogance and his pride and his despicable double-standard that lets him help himself to as many women as he pleases, but allows him to sneer from his golden throne at my sister, who had to make her own way in the world the best she could! He had kept her apart for Andreas, cheated them of what little time they could have had together...*

She sheered her mind away from the dark, familiar thoughts. Recriminations were pointless. The past was gone. Carla was gone, and so was Andreas. Only little Ari remained—and he was happy and content. That was enough. It would have to be.

There was no sign of Nikos Theakis when she and Tina first entered the salon, and Ann was relieved. Tina stepped out on to the terrace with Cousin Eupheme, who was telling her about some new plantings she was planning. Mrs Theakis called Ann to her side, smiling fondly at her.

'I am so glad to see you here at last, my dear. I am more sorry than I can say that so much time has passed without your taking your rightful place in Ari's life,' Mrs Theakis said sadly. Her beautiful dark eyes shadowed. 'I grieved so much,' she went on slowly, 'when Andreas was killed. It is the greatest tragedy of all—to lose a child. That is why, my dear, I begged you for the care of Andreas' son. Holding his child in my arms, I knew God had given me back my own son. You gave me a gift, that day, that I can never repay—'

She stopped, and Ann could see she was near to tears. Impulsively, she took the older woman's thin hand.

'I gave him to you with all my heart,' she said quietly.

There was a footfall, and a voice from the doorway spoke.

'Gave?' questioned Nikos Theakis.

The single word crawled like ice down Ann's spine.

His mother seemed not to hear him. Her face lightened. 'Nikki!' she exclaimed. 'There you are!' She made to get to her feet, and immediately, attentively, her son was there. But even as he moved, he did not stint from casting a look at Ann that might have withered her to the spot.

For the remainder of the evening, until she could retire, as early as she decently could, Ann did her absolute best to minimise the presence of Nikos Theakis. But when, having finally escaped, she stood on the balcony of her room, gazing out over the beautiful nightscape of gardens, beach and sea, emotion seethed in her.

Why do I let him get to me? Why?

It made her angry with herself that she could not ignore him, could not blank him out. She knew what he thought of Carla, what he thought of her—and why should she care? The soft wind winnowed at her hair, lifting it from her nape, making her give a tiny shiver that was not from cold. Why should she care that when she felt that dark, brooding gaze resting on her resentment and intimidation was not all she felt…?

Why could she feel the power of that dark gaze?

The wind came again, playing over her body, sifting her hair with long, sensuous fingers…

No! Her hands clenched over the balustrade. No! She turned away abruptly, heading indoors to make herself ready for bed. But when she lay sleepless, gazing up at the ceiling, that dark, brooding gaze was all that she could see.

CHAPTER THREE

THE NEXT MORNING saw a reprieve. Nikos, so she was informed by his mother over breakfast, had taken himself back to Theakis HQ in Athens. Immediately Ann relaxed, and spent a happy and peaceful three days, devoting herself entirely to Ari. But the following day, visiting Maxos for lunch and some light shopping with Ari and Tina, a helicopter heading out to Sospiris saw Ann's respite from Nikos over.

Worse was to come. The next day was to be an excursion that Ari had been enthusing about several times: a visit to the beach at the far end of the island. To Ann's absolute dismay, Mrs Theakis gave Tina leave to spend the day with her fiancé, and directed Nikos to drive Ann and Ari. Desperately, Ann tried to think of a way to get out of the coming ordeal, but how could she disappoint Ari?

Tense and reluctant, she climbed up with Ari into the canvas-topped Jeep—a mode of transport which had the little boy in transports of delight.

'It's really, really bumpy!' he enthused.

He was not exaggerating. And as Nikos Theakis, who had not yet said a word to her directly, set off at a greater speed than Ann liked along the unmade track heading across the island, she hung on grimly, repeatedly hurled against the metal doorframe as they took hairpin corners and avoided the larger potholes. Finally the Jeep swept to a halt on the stony upper reaches of a beach, and Ann looked around. They had descended into what was almost a hidden valley, between high cliffs that opened out into a patch of close-cropped grazing populated by a handful of goats. The banks of a dry stream bed were smothered in wild oleanders. Beyond, the grass and stones gave way to golden sand and then brilliant azure sea. It was very private, very remote, and incredibly beautiful.

Shakily, Ann got down, lifting Ari with her. He immediately sprinted off on to the beach, as Nikos hefted down a kit bag bulging with beach paraphernalia from the back of the Jeep. As she followed Ari she brushed the chalky dust off her long-sleeved T-shirt and long, loose cotton trousers, shaking out her windblown hair.

'The sea will wash off the dust,' Nikos said laconically beside her, as he fell into step at her side.

She ignored him. She had been doing her best to ignore him ever since the expedition started. Only for Ari's sake and his grandmother's would she be civil to this man. Without their presence she saw no reason to force herself to a hypocritical politeness she did not feel.

Nikos evidently thought otherwise. His hand closed over her arm, stopping her in her tracks. She tried to shake herself free, but his grip was like iron. He turned her towards him and she glared at him balefully. His own dark eyes glinted stonily back at her.

'Understand something. Had I my choice, you would not be here. But my mother wanted this outing to take place, and Ari, as you can see, is deliriously excited. Therefore, for his sake, you will be civil. You will not sulk, or behave badly. Farce it may be, but I will not have Ari upset. Do you understand me?'

'Why else do you think I'm here?' she shot back. 'It's only because of Ari and your mother.'

He stared at her grimly a moment. 'Good,' he said, and let her go, striding off.

She stared after him a moment, rubbing where he'd gripped her arm. A bruise was already coming up from all the bashing it had received on the journey here. She set off again, pausing to take off her canvas shoes as she reached the sand. It was slow progress in the deep soft sand, and by the time she caught up with them Nikos was already making camp in the lee of some rocks to the side of the beach, spreading out a rug over a groundsheet. Ari was helping—if upending the kit bag and rummaging through for spades and buckets could be considered helpful. Finding what he wanted, he immediately started to dig a hole. Ann watched him a moment, a smile playing on her lips. Ari definitely seemed to like his sand holes. As she turned to put her own beach bag down on the rug, she realised that Nikos was watching her, with a different expression from usual on his face. It seemed—assessing.

She busied herself unpacking her bag. She didn't really know what was expected of the day, and had had no intention of asking Nikos, so she had brought what she thought would be likely—including a swimsuit, which she was wearing under her clothes. But not the two-piece. Today's was a workmanlike one piece that was as unrevealing of her figure as a swimsuit could be. Whether she would have the nerve to strip down to it in Nikos Theakis' presence, she didn't know, but she did know that if Ari wanted her to come in the water with him she would not turn him down.

For something to do, and to stop feeling as awkward as she did, she went over to Ari and inspected the progress of his hole so far.

'Would you like me to help?' she offered. It seemed preferable to being stuck with his uncle's company.

Ari shook his head. 'You and Uncle Nikki have to dig your own holes, and the biggest hole wins,' he informed her.

'I'll start one here,' said Ann, moving a little away and dropping to her knees to begin. 'Your uncle can dig his own.'

There was a bite in her words as she spoke that she did not trouble to mute. Nor the unspoken coda—*and bury himself in it too, for all I care!*

She set to, scrabbling at the soft sand until a darker, more compact layer was exposed, which could be dug into satisfactorily. She dug industriously, using her bare hands, pausing only to retie her hair into a pigtail to stop it falling forward.

A shadow fell over her, and then Nikos was hunkering down to inspect both holes.

'Mine is deeper!' claimed Ari.

'You started earlier,' said Nikos. 'And you are using a spade.'

'Auntie Annie can have my spare spade,' said Ari generously, and pushed it across to Ann.

'Auntie Annie…' Nikos's voice was musing.

'Tina has started referring to me as that,' said Ann shortly, reaching for Ari's spare spade and thanking him.

Nikos's eyes rested on her unreadably. 'You do not seem like an "Auntie Annie,"' he said. 'Nor even like a plain and simple "Ann." Surely, once you were able to afford your new wealthy lifestyle, you aspired to a new name to reflect your new image? Even Anna would be more exotic.'

Ann ignored him, merely digging more vigorously.

Nikos levered himself back upright. Why had he let himself bait her like that? It was just that there was something about her today that was galling him more than ever. The intervening days had been intended to put a mental as well as physical distance from her, and though he had had been reluctant to leave her with his mother without his watchful eye, not only had he had things to do in Athens that could not be postponed easily, he'd also wanted a break from Ann Turner.

She was too disturbing to his peace of mind—and not just because of the threat she presented to his family. Ann Turner's presence on Sospiris disturbed him for quite another reason. One he was determined to crush just as ruthlessly as he would crush any attempt on her part to extract yet more money from the Theakis coffers.

While in Athens he had deliberately kept his evenings busy with social events. It was inconvenient, however, that he was currently between affairs. It would have suited him to have someone to take his mind off Ann Turner. She had occupied far too much of it already. Exasperatingly, any hopes that he'd had that when he returned to Sospiris he'd find her considerably less eye-drawing had evaporated on his return. The damn woman had just the same effect on him as before.

It rattled him.

It shouldn't be happening. He knew exactly what she was, and that should be sufficient—more than sufficient!—to put him off her big-time. And yet—

And yet he had found himself once again, covertly watching her—telling himself it was because he was keeping her under surveillance, to show her that every word she uttered was suspect, that he had the measure of her even if she were fooling his mother, and taking in the sculpted line of her jaw, the graceful fall of her hair, the wide-set grey eyes, the sensuous swell of her breasts.

And now it was even worse. His mother had manoeuvred him into taking Ari and the boy's pernicious aunt on this be-nighted jaunt. And for Ari's sake he could not refuse, nor spoil it for him by allowing his hostility to show.

His eyes rested on her bowed head. She was digging away as if possessed, refusing to pay him any attention. And that was another thing—the fact that she wasn't paying him any attention. Deliberately. Conspicuously. She was doing it on purpose, obviously, in an act of defiance—doubtless hoping that it would maybe convince him of a moral purity that was impossible for a woman who had sold her nephew for cash. Her hypocrisy infuriated him.

His mouth set. So Ann Turner, hypocrite and baby-seller, thought she could blank him, did she? Thought she could look through him, cut him, ignore him—defy him? Thought she'd run circles round him by ending up ensconced here, in the lap of luxury, ingratiating herself with his mother, his nephew—the nephew she'd *sold?*

Anger filled him as he watched them—the little boy that was all that was left of the brother he had lost, of the son his mother had lost, and the girl who had valued a million pounds more than an orphaned child, her blood kin. How dared she play the hypocrite? Not just with him, Nikos Theakis, who could see through her hypocrisy, but with the innocent Ari…

Harsh eyes looked at her.

You play with the child you sold to put designer clothes on your back, to jet you around the world…

A memory came back to him—one that filled him with deepest disgust, blackest rage.

Not of Ann Turner.

Of her sister.

A woman who had offered her body for cash—cash from any man who could afford it. Any man rich enough to keep her in the luxury she thought she was worth. Any man…

Bleak, empty eyes looked now on Carla's sister. So, just what was the beautiful, alluring Ann Turner prepared to do to get more money?

His mouth twisted into a travesty of a smile as the thought resolved slowly, temptingly, in his mind. What would she do if he made her an offer he'd make it very, very hard for her to refuse?

Very hard—

For a long moment he just went on looking down at the silvery-gold head. He could feel the blood stirring in his veins as he made his decision. Yes, that was exactly what he would do—make her an offer he would ensure it was impossible for her to refuse, and in so doing take the greatest satisfaction possible himself—in more ways than one! Indulge himself with her exactly as he wanted to. And all in the best possible cause—getting her claws out of his family. Permanently.

Ann sat back and looked at her hole. At least digging it seemed to have shut Nikos Theakis up in his attempts to talk to her.

She looked across at Ari. 'How's it coming?' she enquired.

He paused, and looked across at her. 'Is yours bigger?' he asked.

'I'm not sure,' she temporised.

'Uncle Nikki can judge,' said Ari.

Nikos had, to Ann's relief, returned to the camp, and was idly flicking through a business magazine. Now he looked up, and got to his feet. He strolled across the sand, and Ann did not like to see the way his legs seemed so long in his chinos, or the way his T-shirt moulded to his powerful torso.

Solemnly he inspected both sand holes. 'Ann's is wider, but Ari's is deeper,' he pronounced.

'I win!' shouted Ari excitedly. He turned to his aunt. 'You have to dig them the *deepest*,' he explained. He dropped his spade to the sand. 'Can we swim now, Uncle Nikki—can we?'

He'd spoken in Greek, and Ann could not understand him. Nikos glanced at Ann. 'Well, does your English *sang froid* run to a dip in the Aegean at this time of year?' he enquired laconically.

She gave a shrug. 'I'm happy to go in with Ari,' she said.

As well as not liking the way his legs seemed so long, or his torso so powerful, she also did not like the way he was looking at her. A veiled look that did things to her breathing she did not want it to.

'Good,' he said, and then he said something to Ari which Ann assumed was assent.

She had no objection to taking Ari into the water, however cold it might be. It would get her away from Nikos. He could sit in the sun and read his magazine and welcome. But as she scrambled to her feet, dusting sand off her knees and hands, she froze. Nikos, it seemed, was intending to go in the sea as well.

He was stripping off. Before her frozen eyes, he proceeded to divest himself of his chinos and polo shirt down to bare skin.

She stared, open-mouthed.

His body was fantastic. And there was so much of it! The golden shoulders were just as broad as she'd always known they'd be, his back long and smooth, his legs longer and not smooth—fuzzed with a sheen of dark hair over taut muscles that was echoed in the narrow arrowing above the waistband of his hip-hugging bathing trunks. Whether he worked out or it just came naturally, his abdominal muscles were unblemished by an ounce of fat, and the smooth, olive-hued pectorals were likewise perfect.

As he finished undressing, he glanced at Ann. For a moment his eyes stayed veiled, as if observing her reaction. Then, with an indolent, satisfied smile, he reached out one long index finger under her chin and closed her mouth.

'Your turn,' he invited softly. 'Or should I say—my turn?'

He stood, casually poised, with all the natural grace of a Greek statue but with absolutely none of its Platonic virtues, and waited for her to do likewise and disrobe—so he could watch her the way she had watched him.

As she stood stiff and immobile, he gave her a taunting smile.

'Don't worry, I've checked it out already. You pass muster.'

She started, confused. He enlightened her. 'By the pool. You were sunbathing.'

Colour mounted in her cheek as the penny dropped and subconscious memory flooded back. 'You touched me!' she accused, outraged. God, she thought she'd been dreaming, and all along the hand that she'd imagined stroking over her back had been real. Had been his. Eyes flashing with anger she dropped down to help Ari inflate his armbands and take his T-shirt off.

She heard a mocking laugh, lightly running feet, and then, her eyes automatically flying upwards, she saw Nikos Theakis launching itself into the azure water, splashing loudly in the quietness all around them. As he headed out to sea with long, powerful strokes, Ann dragged her eyes away. Grimly, she helped Ari get ready for swimming.

'You have to come in too!' said Ari.

'After lunch,' she said, sliding his armbands on and checking their fit. 'Anyway, I take ages changing, and Uncle Nikki is already in the water. I'll come and watch you both.'

Accepting this compromise, Ari hammered over the sand to the water's edge, shouting enthusiastically in Greek to the figure cutting through the water. Watching Ari plunge in, and his uncle halt his swimming to meet him, Ann did her best to ignore the way the sunlight played on the hard, lean torso, glistening with water, and on the sleek, slicked back hair and thick, sea-wet eyelashes.

Oh, God, he really is gorgeous to look at…

She felt her stomach hollow out, and not just with dismay…

Deliberately she flicked her gaze to Ari, keeping it fixed on him. Against her will, she had to concede that Nikos Theakis, unspeakable though he was, was a great companion for a four-year-old child. Over and over again he hefted Ari up and tossed him into the sea. Ari yelled with glee. He played chasing games and piggybacking, and aeroplaned him around above the water. Without her realising it, a smile came to her lips as she watched them.

Then they were wading out of the water. Ari was rushing up and giving her a wet hug, describing all the things that

Uncle Nikki and he had done, asking if she'd seen them, and she was taking off his armbands and wrapping his sturdy little body in a towel. At his uncle she did not look at all. Not at all.

But back at the camp she had to, like it or not.

Energy levels quite undimmed by his marine exertions, Ari hopped about from one foot to the other while Ann creamed sun lotion into him. The sun was getting higher now, and even his darker skin tone needed protection.

'Have you cream on your face, Ann?' The question made her look up, and immediately she wished she hadn't.

Nikos was standing, legs apart, his back to the sun, ruffling his hair dry with a towel. He looked—magnificent.

Ann tightened her mouth. 'Yes, I put it on before we set off.'

'You should top up,' Nikos told her. 'Even with your tan you can still burn, and that would ruin that flawless complexion of yours.'

Tight-lipped, Ann applied more sun lotion to herself, knowing the truth of what Nikos had said, despite the way he'd said it. Her complexion was none of his damn business...

Ari tugged at her sleeve. 'It's time to build a sandcastle,' he announced. 'A big one.'

Ann was only too willing. Anything to keep her busy and away from Nikos. She watched as Ari seized his spade and set off to select a good site, just beyond the sand holes, settling down to work. Ann reached for the sun lotion cap and started to screw it on, her eyes focussed on her task—focussed on whatever took her gaze away from where Nikos was lowering himself down with muscular grace on to the rug, leaning back against a large rock, legs stretching out in front of him. Perilously close to her.

But she refused to pull away, calmly returning the sun cream to her beach bag. As she did, Nikos spoke.

'So,' he drawled, 'do you intend to remain covered up neck to ankle the whole day?'

'I've told Ari I'll swim after lunch,' she said. Involuntarily her eyes flickered across to him as she got to her feet.

He lounged back, his drying hair feathering on his forehead, a pair of sunglasses over his nose, swimming trunks hugging his lean hips. The ultimate male. For a helpless moment she could only stare. Could only let him see her stare. Knowing that although she could not see his eyes, his could see her—see her reaction to him.

His mouth curved.

'Look all you want, Ann,' he said generously. 'I'm not going anywhere.' He gave a soft laugh and picked up his magazine again. 'Off you go now,' he said. 'Ari needs a labourer.'

Stiffly, Ann strode off, hating herself.

But not as much as she hated Nikos Theakis.

CHAPTER FOUR

SHE WENT ON hating him for the rest of the day, but she would not spoil it for Ari. Having built his huge and complex castle—a task which Ann had discovered she enjoyed hugely, despite the knowledge that Nikos was only a few metres away, and that Ari regularly invited him to comment approvingly on progress so far—Ari suddenly put down his spade and announced that he was hungry.

It was a general signal for lunch.

They wandered onto the stone terrace of a tiny beach hut which Ann had not even noticed on their arrival. It was set back on the shady side of the beach, above the pebbles, and was pleasantly cool now that the sun was high. Given the Theakis wealth, Ann half expected servants to jump out of nowhere and lay on a four-course luncheon for their lord and master, but their meal in fact came out of a cold bag Nikos had brought with him. It was very simple. A round, flattish loaf of fresh-baked Greek bread, sweet sun-ripe tomatoes, salty, oil-drenched feta cheese, some dry cured ham and a bottle of chilled white wine, with fruit to follow. Ari had a can of cola.

'It's a treat,' he announced smugly to Ann. 'Tina says it rots my teeth so I only have it for treats. Will you be looking after me when Tina marries Dr Sam, Auntie Annie?'

The question slipped out so suddenly that Ann had no time to think up a good answer. Ari's uncle supplied one instead.

'Your aunt isn't used to children, Ari,' he said. 'She wouldn't know how to look after you.'

For a second Ann's expression flickered. She was aware that Nikos was looking at her, a cynical glint in his eye. She ignored it.

'Your uncle is right, Ari,' she said gently. 'I'm sure Ya-ya will find another lovely nanny to look after you. And you'll see Tina still, won't you? She'll only be living on Maxos, and you can visit her in the motor boat.'

'It won't be the same.' His little lip quivered.

'Everything changes, Ari,' said his uncle. 'Some are sad changes, some are happy ones.' There was a strained note in his voice just for a moment.

The boy looked across at Ann. 'You're a happy change, coming to see me,' he said. 'Isn't she, Uncle Nikki?'

Get out of that one, thought Ann silently.

'It has its compensations,' he replied, and his glance flickered over her deliberately. Abruptly, Ann reached for another tomato and bit into it. Her bite was too vicious, and tomato juice and seeds spurted all over her T-shirt.

'Shame,' murmured Nikos Theakis insincerely. 'Now you'll have to take it off after all.'

In the end, she did. The afternoon simply got too hot, and before long Ari was clamouring to go into the sea again. Ann peeled off to her swimming suit, taking advantage of the fact that Nikos was now laying out his fabulous gold-hued body face down on a brilliant white towel for the sun to worship it.

'If you go in the water,' he advised lazily, not bothering to lift his head from the folded towel beneath it, 'don't go out of your depth. No further than that crooked rock to the left. Ari knows which one.'

'Or the sharks will get you,' contributed his nephew knowledgeably, if inaccurately, clearly having been told this to keep him close to shore. 'They lie in wait in deep water.'

Hurriedly she raced Ari down to the sea, welcoming the chill embrace of the water. Playing with Ari took her mind off Nikos, and she entered into his games with enthusiasm, whilst taking care to stay, as instructed, in her depth. Eventually Ari tired, and as they waded out of the sea Ann immediately became aware that she was under professional surveillance.

Nikos Theakis must have seen a multitude of female bodies, but he obviously liked to study each one as a connoisseur. Now he was studying hers, his arms folded behind his neck, using the casual strength of his own perfectly toned, sun-kissed abdominal muscles to hold his head sufficiently off the ground to survey her properly.

Ann attempted to adopt an air of indifference to his scrutiny, and failed. But she did manage to avoid looking at Nikos, instead taking Ari's armbands off and mopping him dry, letting him chatter away in Greek to his uncle before heading back to his sandcastle. Patting herself dry with Ari's towel, Ann knelt down, rummaging in her bag for a comb. Finding it, she straightened, squeezed out the worst of the moisture, and started to comb out her dripping wet hair.

Nikos sat up with an effortless jack-knife of his stomach muscles, hooking his hands loosely around wide splayed knees and looking at her with narrowed eyes, while she tried to look completely indifferent to his regard—and to him. But it was impossible. *He's even got beautiful feet,* Ann thought absently, trying not to look. Narrow, with sculpted arches. She looked away, but he had seen her. He limbered up, and crossed to where she was kneeling. Before she knew what he was doing he'd hunkered down, removed the large-toothed comb from her hand and taken over her task.

'Hold still,' he commanded, as she instinctively tried to get away. A large hand closed over her upper arm. She flinched.

With a frown, he scooped away the wet tangle of hair covering it, revealing the ugly bruise that had formed.

'What the hell?'

'Blame the driver,' she said briefly. 'I got a walloping against the door frame of the Jeep.'

He muttered something in Greek that was probably impolite. 'I'm sorry,' he said tersely. 'I didn't realise.'

She shrugged. 'I'll live,' she answered. 'Give me my comb back.'

He ignored her. Instead, his fingers gently skimmed the smooth skin of her shoulder.

'Your skin is like silk.' His voice was low, intimate. His touch made her shiver. But she didn't feel cold. Heat started to coil in every tensing muscle in her body. For a long moment their eyes met and held—night-dark speculative brown to startled, questioning blue-grey—then, as if in slow motion, Nikos lowered his mouth.

His kiss, on the cusp of her shoulder, was as soft as velvet. Ann's heart stopped beating. Somewhere, in some small, shrinking space, she knew she should jerk away, shout, scream—anything at all to stop what Nikos was so outrageously, unthinkably doing.

But it was impossible. Simply impossible. All she could do, as the world turned inside out, was to stay kneeling, frozen, weak in every limb, feeling the softness of his mouth on her flesh. She felt his lips part, so the soft, liquid warmth of the inside of his mouth was against her tender skin, moving over it, back and forth, moistening and caressing it. Slow bliss filled her. Then gently, very gently, he lifted his head and drew her around so that she was positioned in the vee of his open thighs as he knelt behind her, caging her. With long, even strokes he started to comb out her hair.

She couldn't move. Couldn't move to save her life. Every nerve in her body quivered with awareness. Around her the air hung like silk, shimmering in the heat. As he worked down from her scalp to the still dripping ends of her waist-length hair, gently teasing out every last tangle, she felt a drowsy languor steal over her as the sun beat down. With half closed eyes she could still see little Ari quit his sandcastle to go clambering over the rocks, examining the sea life. Behind her, another Theakis male was seducing her.

She had no doubt that that was what he was doing. Long after the last tangle was gone he went on combing down the length of her hair—soothingly, rhythmically, murmuring soft words in his own native language. It might have been a shopping list for all she knew. She knew it wasn't. He was telling her how much he wanted her, how much his body yearned for hers. How even now—had it not been for the child playing there on the rocks, for the interfering presence of the silky fabric of their bathing clothes—he would have lifted her back on to the hard muscle of his splayed thighs, thigh against thigh, cradling his hips against hers so that she could feel the hardening of his body against her contours.

He would take her soft breasts in the palms of his hands and caress them until her nipples hardened like peaks, and then he would roll them in his long fingers until she cried out, tiny moans in her throat that told him she was ready. Then his hand would splay down over the soft swell of her belly to ease her firm thighs apart, exposing the very heart of her, and he would let his clever, skilful fingers explore her secret folds until they found the pathway to delight. They would rouse her to such a point of glistening ecstasy that her back would arch away from him, her head would drop back, exposing the long line of her tender throat, which he would kiss and bite with soft, devouring kisses while her cry of ecstasy reverberated against his mouth as he possessed her with his body…

Ann felt the heat pool between her thighs and begin to

quicken. Her breasts tautened, nipples peaking beneath the damp swimsuit. Her head started to drop as the murmuring voice told her of all the delights he would give her, and her scalp tingled at the touch of the comb he wielded so soothingly. So arousingly.

Her body began to melt against his waiting hardness.

In slow motion she saw the little figure at the edge of her vision reach the top of the highest rock and wave triumphantly. Then, as her eyes widened in shock, she saw him wobble, arms flailing wildly, and start to tumble.

Which of them moved faster she didn't know. Ann only knew that she had hurled herself forward like a bullet from a gun, scrambling desperately over the rocks to try and break Ari's fall. She caught at him, gasping out words.

'I've got you. I've got you. You're safe.'

Then Ari was slithering down through her weakened arms, before being halted again by a pair of much stronger, harder arms, scooping him out of Ann's, holding his kicking, frightened little body against a broad, strong chest. Rapid Greek urgently reassured the child, soothing him.

Carefully, Nikos lowered the crying child down to a towel. Swiftly the pair of them examined him for damage, but apart from a nasty scrape down one calf Ari seemed nothing more than shocked. And being fussed over, plus a packet of crisps, soon put his woes behind him.

'Tina will put a plaster on it,' he informed his aunt and uncle as he inspected his scrape again, crunching crisps as he spoke.

'It won't need one, poppet,' Ann said reassuringly. 'It isn't bleeding.'

'It bleeds if I squeeze it,' Ari corrected her, and proceeded to demonstrate the truth of this with ghoulish pleasure.

Ann looked away, meeting Nikos' eye. For a moment a gleam of mutual humour passed between them, then he looked back at his nephew.

'Repellent boy,' he said.
Ari looked pleased.

The journey back to the villa was conducted at a far more sedate pace than their outward journey. Nikos was deaf to Ari's pleas to speed up, and took the rough road slowly this time.

'Thank you,' said Ann stiffly, conscious that Nikos had driven slowly for her.

She was still shaken. Not because of Ari's fall—though that had been a horribly sobering moment. Because of what had preceded it. *How* the *hell* had it happened? In the space of a handful of seconds she'd gone from being in control of herself to being...

Helpless. Completely helpless to do anything at all except let the extraordinary velvet seduction of the man take her over completely. Fatally. Lethally.

The moment the Jeep was back at the villa she was out of it, extracting Ari as fast as she could. To her relief, Nikos kept the engine running, and the moment Ari was down drove straight off round to the villa's garages. Ari, seizing Ann's hand, headed indoors, where he was intercepted by Maria, the nursery maid, who exclaimed dutifully at Ari's grievous wound, then whisked him off to get cleaned up. Gratefully, Ann escaped to her room. Under a punishingly hot shower she mercilessly berated herself. How *could* she have let Nikos Theakis do that to her? Touch her, caress her, kiss her...

And why had he done it? But she knew, with a hollowing damning of herself. It had been a power play, pure and simple. He'd done it deliberately, calculatingly, just to show her that he could. To show that she would succumb because he could make it impossible for her not to! That she was powerless against him...

I can't let him have that kind of power! I can't!

No—she had to fight it. And at least now, she told herself

urgently, in her head, she was now prepared for his new battle against her. He'd shown his hand, made his move, and that meant he could no longer launch a surprise attack on her the way he'd done on the beach. She was forewarned now, and that meant forearmed. All she had to do was be on her absolute guard against him.

Whatever it took.

Because the alternative was—unthinkable.

Nikos stared at his reflection in the bathroom mirror of his self-contained apartment in the villa, his razor stilled in one hand.

He was playing with fire.

His mouth tightened. That was the only word for it. He hadn't thought it would be. Had thought it would simply be a matter of killing two birds with one very satisfying stone— gratifying the increasingly persistent desire to enjoy a woman he wanted whilst simultaneously ensuring that Ann Turner was led very nicely up the garden path to a position where she could be ejected, once and for all, from his family.

But that incident on the beach had proved otherwise. Had proved that he was, indeed, playing with fire in what he was doing.

I was out of control so much I didn't even notice when Ari was in danger.

The words formed in his head, sobering and grim. A warning, clear as a bell. And one he would be insane not to heed.

Whatever Ann Turner had, he had to ensure that the only person who got burnt was her. Not him.

With controlled, precise strokes, he started to shave.

Outside the door to the salon, Ann paused. She could feel her chest was tight, her nerves taut. She wanted to bolt back to her room, but it was impossible. She had to get through this evening—the rest of her time on Sospiris. Ignoring completely the man who'd turned her into a quivering, sensuous, conscienceless fool.

Gritting her teeth, she walked in.

Her eyes went to him immediately, sucked to him. Her stomach hollowed, taking in, in a devastating instant, the way he stood there, casually dressed in dark blue trousers, open necked shirt, freshly shaved, lifting his martini glass to his mouth, his unreadable eyes resting on her. For a second so brief it hardly existed she felt his gaze make contact. Then it was gone. His attention was back on Tina, who was talking about archaeology.

Smiling awkwardly, Ann went across to Mrs Theakis and Cousin Eupheme.

How she got through dinner she wasn't sure, but she managed it somehow. Inevitably the conversation included a discussion of the day's expedition, and Ann had to fight the colour seeking to mount in her cheeks. Her comments were disjointed, and in the end she pleaded a headache from too much sun, and fled back to her room before coffee was served. She felt Nikos Theakis's dark gaze on her as she left the dining room.

For the next two days Ann stuck to Tina and Ari like glue. It was easy enough. The following day Ari had a playdate on Maxos, with the young son of wealthy friends of the Theakises, and after handing him over to the family's nanny at their sumptuous holiday villa, Tina took Ann off to spend the afternoon at the dig her fiancé was directing, before heading back to collect Ari again. That evening she was relieved to discover that Nikos was out.

'He is dining with the family that little Ari spent the day with,' said Mrs Theakis, when Ann joined her. 'One of their house guests has a *tendre* for him,' she said dryly. She looked directly at Ann. 'My son is very… popular with our sex, my dear. He has much of what they want. Most noticeably, considerable wealth.' Was there the slightest snap in her voice as she spoke? Ann wondered. Then another thought crossed her mind—a horrible one.

Is she warning me off? She felt cold at the thought.

'And so handsome, too!' This from Cousin Eupheme, who had, Ann had already observed, a visible soft spot for Nikos Theakis.

'Yes,' allowed Mrs Theakis. 'It is a dangerous combination. For him, that is. A man who is both rich and handsome.' Again she looked directly at Ann, and now Ann knew that indeed she was being specifically warned. 'Such a man can be tempted not to treat women with the respect they should have from him.'

Ann stared. This was not what she had thought Mrs Theakis had been going to say.

Mrs Theakis continued, in the same gentle, contemplative voice she always used. 'I would hesitate to call my own son spoilt, and yet— Ah, Yannis—*epharisto!*' This last to the manservant, who had approached with the customary tray of pre-dinner drinks.

To Ann's relief, the subject of the conversation turned, with Mrs Theakis asking Ann what she had made of both Tina's fiancé's dig and her fiancé himself. Tina was still with Sam, Ann having brought Ari back to Sospiris on her own. Ari had been full of his enjoyable adventures on his play-date—except for one aspect.

'She kept kissing me, and I did not like it!' he'd complained.

'Who was that?' Ann had asked, amused.

'A grown-up lady. She asked me about Uncle Nikki. I said he was busy working. That is what he tells Yannis to tell ladies when they phone him. I told *her* that too. She did not like it and went away. I was glad. I didn't like her kissing me.' He looked at Ann. 'Uncle Nikki does not kiss. He hugs. And he carries me on his shoulders. *If,*' he'd added, punctiliously, 'I do not pull his hair.'

Now, over dinner, Ann wondered what Ari's admirer was like. She would be elegant and well bred—one of his own circle. As socially acceptable as Carla, Ann thought darkly, had *not* been suitable to marry into the wealthy Theakis family.

There was no sign of Nikos the following day, or the one thereafter, and Ann assumed that he was still on Maxos. But wherever he was—providing it was not on Sospiris—she couldn't care less. It was taking all her strength, even with him not around, to force herself not to think about what had happened on the beach. But it was essential to banish the memory—vital not to think about Nikos Theakis. Not to conjure his image in her mind. Not to let him into her consciousness. To think of something else—anything else—that would take her mind into safer pathways again.

She was glad when Tina returned mid-morning, bearing with her an invitation to join her and her fiancé for the birthday celebrations of one of Sam's colleagues the following night.

'You will come, won't you?' Tina pressed. 'Oh, it won't be anything grand like here, of course, but it will be good fun, I promise!'

Mrs Theakis added her own urging. 'My dear—young people, and a lovely, lively evening for you!' She smiled her warm, kind smile at Ann.

So, in the early evening of the next day, she set off with Tina to cross the strait to Maxos in the Theakis launch. Ari had been consigned to Maria's care, and mollified with the reminder that the following day his playdate friend was coming over to Sospiris on a return invitation. Tina was looking very pretty, with her curly brown hair, and was wearing a flirty red sundress jazzed up with some locally crafted jewellery. Ann was a fair-haired foil, with an ivory-white lacy cross-over top and a floaty turquoise skirt which she'd bought the day they'd come over to Maxos between with Ari.

Sam met them at the harbour, his eyes dwelling with open

appreciation on his fiancée and with practised masculine appreciation on Ann's pale beauty. Gallantly, he offered an arm to each, and they started to stroll towards the quayside lined with tavernas. The Theakis launch had dropped them at the marina end of the harbour, which was visibly upmarket—as were the gleaming yachts at moorage and the smart bars along this section of the quayside. At that hour of the evening, with the dusk gathering in the sky and the last pale bars of daylight dying in the west, both Greeks and such tourists as there were at that season were making their traditional *volta*—the slow procession of both seeing and being seen.

Sam and Tina paused to greet acquaintances as they passed, and halfway along stopped more decisively when they were hailed by a party sitting outside a particularly smart cocktail bar.

Nikos Theakis had hailed them—sitting back, looking relaxed, his shirt open at the collar, a sweater loosely draped over broad shoulders, long legs extended, glass in his hand. A very elegant, sultry-looking brunette was sitting close enough beside him on the white cushioned padded cane seat to signal that her physical proximity to him was usually a lot closer.

'Tina,' said Nikos with smiling extravagance, his white teeth gleaming wolfishly, 'you're looking stunning tonight. Sam's a lucky man.' His dark eyes paid tribute to her, before moving on to exchange pleasantries with her fiancé. Then, without warning, his gaze flicked to Ann.

She'd been standing stiffly, trying to act normally, trying not to be instantly, horribly, mega-aware of Nikos Theakis's impact. She had been quite unprepared for this, and was desperately scrabbling for her guard.

Too late. Those dark long-lashed eyes rested on her, and sucked hers into his gaze.

For a blinding moment it felt intimate—shockingly, searingly intimate. As if there was no one else there at all. As if his eyes were branding her.

Then, abruptly, his head turned towards the woman at his side, whose hand, Ann slowly registered, was now curved possessively around his forearm.

'Nikos, darling,' she announced in overloud English, 'we mustn't keep your nephew's nanny and her friends from their evening out—you'll lose your reputation for being such a generous employer to your household staff!'

At her side, Ann could feel Sam tense with anger at this dismissive put-down of his fiancée.

'True,' Sam said with deceptive ease. 'But one must, of course, also be careful not to *gain* reputations, either—such as one for hunting rich husbands, Kyria Constantis.'

He bestowed a sardonic smile on the woman, whose expression darkened furiously, and strode off, taking his fiancée and Ann with him. Only Ann, it seemed, registered the low chuckle that emanated from Nikos Theakis, and the hiss of outrage from his companion at the scarcely veiled insult.

'Isn't Elena Constantis a complete cow?' Tina quizzed Ann, visibly pleased that her fiancé had supported her so ruthlessly.

'Nikos doesn't seem to think so,' retorted Ann. She was still trying to recover from that scorching eye contact—which had seared so effortlessly through the guard she'd barely had time to scrabble for—and she was also trying to ignore the fact that she had seen Nikos Theakis cosying up to another woman.

Too late she caught the fatal admission she'd just made. Using the word 'another'....as if she herself had *anything* to do with the man in that way.

Tina was speaking again, and Ann latched on to the diversion. Unfortunately, she was still on the same subject.

'Oh, Nikos won't marry Elena Constantis—however much she wants him to. Apart from anything else he'd never marry someone Ari didn't approve of, and Ari's made it clear he doesn't like Elena Constantis. He says she keeps trying to kiss him.'

Ann felt her spirits lift illogically, though she knew there was absolutely no reason for it. She made herself remember that as they reached the taverna where Sam's colleagues were gathering. She was glad of the party. The mix of professional archaeologists and students was a lively, polyglot gathering, and the taverna in the old port was a world away from the swish marina. Not a place for a Theakis, thought Ann, and found the thought reassuring.

As the evening wore on, and the local wine went round, she felt herself relaxing. It was good to get away from the constant threat of encountering Nikos, from keeping her guard high, as she must around him.

The convivial meal culminated in a large birthday cake, with ouzo, brandy and coffee doing the rounds, followed by some very inexpert and woozy dancing to bouzoukis. It was all very good humoured, but finally the taverna owner could bear it no longer. With a clap of his hands he banished them all back to their table, and summoned the males of his establishment, who obligingly formed the appropriate line in front of their enthusiastic audience.

A voice in Greek from the doorway halted them. Ann looked round. Half shadowed against the night, a tall figure peeled itself away from the entrance.

The taverna owner hurried forward, exclaiming volubly in his own language, and held out his arms welcomingly.

Nikos Theakis strolled in.

CHAPTER FIVE

ANN WAS SITTING sandwiched between Tina and one of Sam's colleagues, and as she realised what was happening she felt her stomach hollow.

It was the last thing she had expected. The last thing she had been prepared for.

What is he doing here?

The question ricocheted through her like an assassin's bullet shot out of nowhere. Then something else fired straight through her. Far worse than shock. She could feel it in every nerve-ending in her skin, every synapse in her wine-inflamed brain. It was a quickening of her breath, her pulse, making her instantly, totally aware of him as if everyone else in the taverna had ceased to exist. Dismay washed through her, but it was too late—far too late. All she could do was gaze helplessly at him, as he raised a hand in casual greeting to Sam and the others and made some remark in Greek to the taverna owner. The latter smiled vigorously, and gestured Nikos further in. The honoured guest murmured his thanks, casually deposited his sweater on a spare chair, and took his place in the row of men.

The music started again.

The hypnotic thrum of the music started to reverberate through the room, and very slowly the line of men, shoulder to shoulder, started to weave to the soft, but intensely rhythmic music. Hypnotically, the music started to quicken, becoming insistent, mesmerising. Overpowering.

Ann watched, feeling her heart swelling. Even without the presence of Nikos Theakis she would have been riveted by the unconscious grace, the intense dignity, the suffused sensuality of the dancers. These men dancing were real men. Every one of them. Masculinity and virility radiated from each of them, from the oldest white-haired elder to the youngest teenage grandson. As their interlinked bodies stepped with flawless unison through the paces Ann could feel the tension mount, excitement thrum in the air.

It was a magnificent sight. And none so magnificent than that of Nikos Theakis, dancing like one of his own ancestors, binding the stones of Greece to the wine-dark sea of Homer, grace and power and sensuality personified.

In the subdued light his white shirt gleamed like a sail, its open collar exposing the powerful column of his throat and his raised arms, embracing the shoulder of the man next to him in the line stretching the material over his muscled torso. The way his dark head turned, the way his long legs flexed and stepped—Ann felt her stomach clench. He was stunningly, overpoweringly beautiful. Heat flowed through her body. She couldn't take her eyes off him. Not for a moment, not for a second. She didn't care if people saw her looking. Didn't care if Nikos Theakis saw her watching him. And if his eyes met hers, held them completely, totally, never letting her go, as if she were their captive…

It was as if he were dancing for her, displaying his prowess, his masculinity, for her alone…

She felt dazed—dazzled and aware.

Responding to him. Weakening to him.

As the music and the dance reached its rampant finale to a volley of applause and vociferous appreciation by its audience, she dropped her head, shaken with what she was feeling. Yet there was still that quickening in her veins that seemed to make the whole world more vivid.

She lifted her head again, and her eyes clashed straight into his.

He had joined the party at the table, finding a space, somehow, immediately opposite her. For a moment—how long or brief it was she could not tell—he simply held her gaze.

Then he was accepting a glass of brandy from the taverna owner, exchanging something with him in Greek which brought a comment from Sam in the same language. Nikos made an airy gesture with his free hand, lounging back in his seat.

'It is my pleasure—a token of appreciation for all the hard work you and your team put in on the excavation,' he said smoothly, and Ann gathered that he'd picked up the tab for the evening.

It brought back the question that had originally struck her when he'd strolled in. Why was he here? Why wasn't he with the elegant, chic Elena Constantis? And where was she? She would not have relinquished her prize easily. And why should Nikos have relinquished her?

He wasn't looking at her now, and she was grateful. He was talking across the table to Sam and a couple of his colleagues, asking them about progress on the dig. She dragged her eyes away, occupying herself with drinking her coffee until the party finally broke up. Outside, after the warmth of the taverna, the night air struck chill. But Ann was glad of it. There was enough heat in her body.

Her blood.

Yet the fresh air seemed to bring on an increase in the effects of her evening's consumption of wine. Where was Tina? She looked around, but Tina was standing beside Sam, who had his arm around her.

'I've told Tina she can stay here with Sam,' said a deep, accented voice behind her.

She turned abruptly. Nikos was draping his sweater casually around his shoulders. 'I'll see you back to Sospiris,' he said to her.

Where her stomach had been, a hollow opened up. Dismay filled it. And something else. Something she really, really didn't want—

Her hands clutched at her bag. 'No, really—that's quite unnecessary,' she began, flustered.

But her protest was ignored. Nikos was saying something to the taverna-owner again. And when she looked pleadingly at Tina the other girl was grinning delightedly up at Sam. Ann felt the words die on her lips. Of course Tina would be pleased that her boss had given her the night off! How selfish would it be to expect her to give that up? And it was only a short journey across on the launch. She could survive that.

But why was Nikos Theakis coming back to Sospiris anyway? Why wasn't he with Elena Constantis?

Mentally, she shook herself. *Who cares? What does it matter? It's nothing to do with me! I've just got to tough it out and get to the other side, that's all.*

'Ready?'

A hand was on her spine. Large, warm. Its heat reached through her thin top. She jerked forward, managing to get out a last 'goodnight' to Tina and Sam and the others, who were heading back to their accommodation on the edge of the town. Then the hand was pressing into her back, urging her forward. She took a jerky step and started walking. The hand dropped.

Self-consciousness possessed her. She felt dangerously affected by the wine, the chill evening air in her lungs—the heat in her veins. Her pulse seemed to have the hypnotic rhythm of the bouzouki music in it still. Yet, though she felt hot, she shivered.

'Wait,' said Nikos beside her, unknotting his sweater,

draping it around her shoulders like a shawl. She felt his body heat in the fabric.

'No—I—'

He ignored her protest, starting to walk on again along the harbour's edge. There were still a few people around, but most of the restaurants were shut, only some of the bars open. Lights played on the dark water, and out at the end of the quay Ann could make out the harbour lights, marking the entrance. She could see the Theakis launch at its mooring, and as they neared a figure stood up from a bench, extinguished a cigarette, and greeted his boss in Greek. Nikos returned the greeting laconically, and stepped down into the launch, holding his hand to help Ann in. Reluctantly she took it, letting go of it again as soon as possible. She took her seat, tucking her skirt around her and holding on to the sleeves of Nikos' sweater.

It seemed strangely, disturbingly intimate to be wearing it like that.

The engine was gunned, roaring to life, and they were nosing out into the harbour. Ann felt the wind lift at her hair as they picked up speed, and she reached up a hand to hold it back. At least, she thought gratefully, the noise of the engine made it hard to speak. But awareness of Nikos' presence beside her dominated her. For something to do, she gazed up at the sky, looking at the bright stars. Abruptly the launch hit a swell, side on, and bucked. Caught off balance, Ann jerked in her seat. Immediately the hand was back on her spine, steadying her. She stiffened instantly, reaching for the gunwale, waiting for the hand at her back to drop.

But it stayed where it was.

'Thank you, but I'm fine now,' she said tightly.

'Focus on the horizon. You won't feel dizzy then,' said Nikos. He had leant towards her, to speak above the noise of the engine.

She gritted her teeth, doing as he bade. Ahead of them the dark mass of Sospiris gradually grew closer. But horribly, horribly slowly. The hand was still at her spine, but she would not, *would not,* tell him to take it away. Would not pay him any attention. Would completely ignore him.

It was impossible to ignore the presence of Nikos Theakis beside her, his hand at her back, even though she was straining away from him as much as she could. His long legs were braced, one arm stretched out along the gunwale. Impossible to ignore the subtle scent of him—a mix of brandy, expensive aftershave, and something more. A scent of masculinity...

Never had the crossing seemed to take so long.

At her side, Nikos wondered to himself whether he were insane.

The evidence was certainly in favour of that judgement. Ever since he'd looked himself in the eye in his bathroom mirror and told himself he was playing with fire, he'd known what the smart thing to do would be. It would be to take full advantage of the fortuitous presence of Elena Constantis— even if it did only fuel her ambitions. It did not, most *definitely* did not, include what he'd done this evening, seeking Ann out. What he was doing right now.

Let alone what he wanted to do...

He dragged his mind away. He shouldn't be here—he knew that. He shouldn't have murmured insincere apologies to Elena, ignoring the snap of frustrated anger in her eyes. He shouldn't have found his steps taking him in the direction of the old port, shouldn't have found himself outside the taverna where he'd known the archaeologists would be. And when he'd heard the familiar, hypnotic, compelling age-old music coming out of the doors and windows he definitely should not have gone inside. And when he'd gone inside he should never have succumbed to the impulse to join in the dancing.

And he should never have allowed himself the pleasure of watching Ann Turner unable to tear her eyes away from him…

But that was just what he had allowed himself to do—and why? Because he'd wanted to. He'd seen her, and wanted her.

Very simple. Very stupid.

Wasn't that why he'd been avoiding the girl as much as he could since the afternoon on the beach, spending time instead with Elena? He was playing with fire again. Because that incident had shown him vividly, urgently, that his grand plan for her was far too incendiary—for him. Yes, seducing the girl and keeping her as his mistress would be an excellent way of getting rid of her, spiking her guns, but the seduction had to be one way only. *He* would be seducing *her*—*not* the other way round. That was essential. He and he alone had to be calling the shots.

More logic impressed itself upon him impeccably, giving him exactly the answers he wanted to questions he didn't want to ask in the first place. He spelt it out to himself. It was exactly because Ann Turner was what she was—a woman who would sell her own sister's baby for cash—that he had fought his attraction to her. Of course he had! She was the very last woman he should sully himself with—however deceptively beautiful her packaging. But it had been precisely *because* he'd fought his attraction to her that it was now so powerful. He could see it with absolute clarity. Logic carried him forward inexorably. Which therefore meant that his reaction to her on the beach had been so extreme only because he'd been trying to suppress his attraction to her. And so now, if he simply gave free rein to his desire, stopped trying to suppress it, his reaction to her would be nothing more than what he was familiar with, comfortable with. The normal reaction he had to a woman he found sexually enticing…

Satisfaction eased through him. Problem analysed. Problem solved. He wanted Ann Turner. There were very good reasons for permitting himself to do so—and no good reason for denying himself what he wanted.

A highly pleasurable bedding. Followed by an equally satisfying removal of a thorn in his side. Once Ann Turner was his mistress, his mother would not invite her to Sospiris again...

His eyes moved over her. She was all unseeing of him. Beneath his palm the fine material of her top fluttered in the wind. Almost he pressed his hand forward, to feel the warmth of her flesh soft beneath his palm, the heat of her pliant body. For nothing more than an instant unease ghosted through his mind as the dark mass of Sospiris loomed closer and the launch came in under its lee, heading to the quay.

Then it was gone. Stavros cut the throttle, nosing the craft forward until he could reach for the mooring. They were back at Sospiris, and the night—Nikos got easily to his feet to alight, holding down his hand to Ann—the night had scarcely begun.

CHAPTER SIX

WITH DEEP RELUCTANCE Ann took the outstretched hand. It was warm, and large, and the strong fingers folded over hers effortlessly, drawing her up on to the stone quay. For a few seconds she felt unsteady, after the rocking of the boat, and yet again she stiffened as his hand moved to her spine again, performing the dual office of steadying her and impelling her forward with smooth pressure.

'Mind the steps,' his low voice reminded her. It was not a drawl, precisely, but it was lazily spoken, with a note to it that she was deeply aware of.

His hand was there again, and though with any other man it would not have signified anything other than common courtesy, with Nikos she knew it was quite, quite different. It was his brand on her. A brand that went right through the thin layer of her top.

In deafening silence she walked up the steps, gained the level ground at the top as he guided her through the stone archway that led into the main gardens. She went docilely, as if there was nothing awkward in the slightest about Nikos Theakis walking through the villa's midnight gardens, with the scent of jasmine and honeysuckle filling the night air so that her breath caught the scent, rich and fragrant.

'Eupheme planted them there deliberately,' Nikos remarked.

'So that you walk, as it were, into a wall of scent at just that point. The night air always gives so much more intense a fragrance, does it not?'

He paused on a little stone concourse, where massed vegetation softened the stone walls, the tiny white flowers of jasmine like miniature stars beneath the sky. Another, wider, shallower flight of stone steps led down from here into the garden spreading away below, and where they stood was a vantage point over the whole expanse. Without realising it, Ann paused as well, automatically taking in the landscaped vista beyond, from the artfully winding pathways, the sculpted vegetation, the little walls festooned in bougainvillea, their brilliant hues dimmed now, and out towards the stand of cypress trees at the garden's far edge, their narrow forms spearing the night sky.

There was no moon, but starlight gleamed on the sea beyond, and caught, too, the iridescent surface of the swimming pool, nestled into its terrace between the villa and the garden.

Ann gazed out over the vista. 'It really is beautiful,' she said. It was impossible not to say so. Impossible not to stand there drinking it in and feel the heady intoxication of the flowers' fragrance, the even headier intoxication of her blood. She wasn't sure how much wine she had drunk—she could feel it suffusing her veins, feel it swirling gently through her—but it seemed to have put the world into a strange, seductive blend whereby she seemed both supersensitive to everything around her and yet everything seemed dissociated from her, unreal almost…as if she were drifting through it like a veil.

But she knew she should not go on standing here beside Nikos, gazing out over the starlit garden with the scent of flowers in her nostrils, the soft music of the cicadas playing in the vegetation. She should, in fact, walk briskly away along the stone pathway to the terrace and get inside the villa, go

straight to her bedroom. Where, equally briskly, she should
take off her make-up, brush out her hair, get into her night-
dress, get into bed, and go peacefully, immediately to sleep.

That, she knew, was precisely what she should do. Right now.

Not stand here in the soft Aegean night, feeling the wine
whispering in her head, feeling the dark, solid presence of
Nikos Theakis standing beside her. His hand was still grazing
her back, so close that all she had to do was turn slightly
towards him to let that warm, strong hand press her against
him, to let her hand splay against the fine cotton of his shirt,
feeling the hard wall of his chest beneath as she lifted her gaze
to him, to drink in the shadowed planes of his face, the dark
sweep of lashes across those eyes that could sear right through
her, making her breath catch in her throat, making her sway,
as if she were a flower on the breeze. His arm would encircle
her pliant body, and his sensual, sculpted mouth would come
down on hers—

She jerked forward—a single step. But it was enough to
shake her back to reality.

'I must go in,' she said. Her voice sounded abrupt. She
gazed at the long façade of the villa, brow furrowing slightly.
Where, exactly, was she to get inside?

'This way.' His voice was smooth, assured.

Automatically she went the way he indicated, walking
slightly in front of him until the path converged on the main
terrace. Even though she had broken the moment, she still
seemed to be in that state of hypersensitivity, feeling his
presence behind her in every follicle in her body. Yet to everything else she seemed quite blind. So much so that when
he stepped past her, to halt her progress and slide open the
French window they were adjacent to, indicating she should
step through, she did so.

And stopped. This was not a salon or a hallway, or any
room she was familiar with.

It was a bedroom.

She turned. Nikos was smoothly sliding shut the French window again.

And walking towards her.

She stepped backwards. It was automatic, instinctive.

'What—?'

He gave a low, brief laugh. 'Don't be naïve, Ann. What do you think?' There was amusement in his voice.

He came up to her, looking down at her. There was a single low lamp burning by the bed—a wide double bed, swathed in a dark coverlet, sombre and masculine—dimmed right down. By its light his face seemed more planed than ever, with shadows etching his features. She felt weak suddenly, overcome. Gazing at him, lips parting.

Her breath quickened.

He saw it, saw her reaction. Saw how it came even without conscious volition.

'This has been waiting for us since the beach,' he said, his voice low, with a timbre that she could feel in her spine. 'Then was not the time—but now... Now, Ann, we have all the time we need.'

Dark long lashes swept down over her. He reached forward, his hands closing over the loose arms of his sweater, still draped around her shoulders. She had long ceased to be conscious of it, having had so much else to dominate her awareness, but now she was vividly aware of it again, and even more vividly, breathlessly aware of the slight but inexorable pull he exerted through the sleeves, around her neck and shoulders.

Drawing her forward.

For a moment, a balance of time she could not say lasted either a few fleeting seconds or a long, long interval of consciousness, she felt herself resist. Felt her mind fill with the realisation that she must step back again and flee to the door behind her. Flee away from this man on whom her eyes were fixed as he drew her casually towards him, until he was discarding the sweater, sliding his hands along the slender column of her torso, his fingers splaying around her ribs. Sensation rippled down her as her breath caught again, mouth parting yet again, as she felt his thumb grazing the swelling underside of her breasts.

He held her there, in position for him, as his hooded gaze held hers, and he casually, leisurely, let his thumbs glide across the tautening material of her top.

She felt her nipples flower, the delicate tissues of her breasts engorge. And he felt it too, for he gave a smile. Slow and sensual. Watching her reaction.

'Very nice, Ann,' he murmured. 'Very nice indeed. As is this…' he continued, in the same considering tone.

His mouth came down in slow and sensual possession. As if he had every right to taste her, every right to let his lips smooth over hers, explore their contours, then ease them apart to taste the nectar within. Every right to overwhelm all her senses and render her helpless, unresisting, capable of nothing except feeling the exquisite sensuality of his kiss, tasting her, possessing her…arousing her…

She could feel the blood surge in her veins like a hot tide, drowning out everything. Everything except what was happening. Nikos Theakis was kissing her…holding her… seducing her…

She knew it was happening, but she could not stop it. It was too overpowering, too overwhelming. All rational thought, such as was left, was gone—dissolved away. All that existed was sensation—sweet, arousing, seductive. She could no more resist it than honey poured over a hot spoon could resist melting.

He let her go, and for a moment she only swayed blindly, held in his sensual grip. Then his hands were sliding around her spine, unfastening the tie of her crossover top, drawing each section of the lacy fabric away to reveal her bra beneath, straining over her engorged breasts. Smoothly he eased the top from her, over each shoulder, discarding it carelessly. Then his hands were at her spine again, slipping the fastening of her bra.

Her swollen breasts fell free, her bra following her top to the floor, and she was standing there, bared to the waist, the coral peaks of her nipples full and erect.

Dark eyes washed over her, flaring as they did so.

'Perfect,' he murmured. 'Quite, quite perfect...'

With a leisurely motion he lifted his hand, letting the backs of his fingers drift against the fullness of the twin orbs. She gave a low, incoherent moan in her throat, her eyes fluttering as the exquisite sensation he aroused shimmered through her. A low laugh came from him.

'Oh, Ann—do you have any idea how disturbing your breasts have been to my peace of mind? And now—now I can have my fill of them.'

His fingers drifted over them again, gently scissoring her nipples. The low moan in her throat came again. Heat beat up in her, and she felt her breasts react more strongly still, straining forward, as if eager for his touch. Her mind was in meltdown—inchoate, formless, distilled to pure, exquisite sensation and the heady, erotic knowledge that she was standing here, naked to the waist, while Nikos Theakis caressed the breasts he had bared for his pleasure.

Another low moan came from her parted lips, and this time it was as a signal to him. He swept her up, her skirt trailing to the floor, swung her around and then lowered her down on to the bed. Her hands splayed upwards, above her head, lifting her breasts, and for a moment he just gazed down on her, his eyes narrowed to a beam of intense focus that quickened the blood in her, susurrated on her skin. She could only lie there, gazing up at him, letting her eyes twine with his, letting the desire flaring in them accentuate her own desire so that it flooded out all the last, fleeing shards of her resistance, drowned them out. Her desire was all-possessing, all consuming—to reach for that tall, strong body looming over her, to close her hands over the sinewed arms, draw it down to her, feel its hard muscled weight press down on her...

'Nikos—'

Where had that word come from, murmuring from her lips? Had she really spoken his name. Pleaded it? Invited it—?

Invited *him?*

Invited him to do what he was doing now—stripping the clothes from his body so that her eyes widened, as they had widened once before on the beach, as his flawless body was revealed to her. Her eyes gloried in his arrant masculinity and his eyes never left hers, never strayed from the body she was displaying for him. Prepared now, he lowered himself down beside her, his hand splaying once more over each breast, his body moving over hers, his mouth finding hers.

He renewed his possession skilfully, expertly, with lips and tongue, soft and gliding, arousing and desiring. He drew from her a response she had not known was possible, engendered a sensuous bliss she had not known existed till that moment. His hands explored her body, turning it in his strong, assured grasp, unwinding her from her long skirt until she was boneless beneath him, until her body was a mesh of arousal. His hands smoothed over her, making him master of every portion of her body, easing her thighs apart, long, skilled fingers teasing the delicate folds concealed.

She gasped in pleasure, her head rolling back into the softness of the pillow, lips parting as the breath exhaled from her. She heard him give a low laugh, and then his lips were almost at hers, and he was teasing them with his even as his hand was performing the same office between her thighs, teasing the dewing flesh.

He murmured something to her, but she was beyond hearing, beyond anything but drowning in the sensations he was engendering. She moaned again, fingers clenching into the pillow as his fingers began their skilful, unbearable work. He eased her thighs yet further apart, gained deeper access to her, finding the throbbing nub of her desire. Arousingly he caressed it as her breath quickened to gasping, her body threshing in a flux of desire as he arched over her, his hand sliding away from her, letting the tip of his manhood take its place. Instinctively, blindly, her hands splayed over his hard, taut buttocks, holding him there, and her hips lifted to him in a gesture as old as time. Her mouth was questing against his, her breasts straining against the muscled wall of his chest, her peaked nipples crushed against it.

Fire licked through her. Her body was aflame, aching for his possession. She strained against him and his mouth was lifting from hers, saying something. She knew not what, but there was promise in it, promise and purpose…

Her head threshed from side to side as wave after wave of pleasure broke through her. She cried out, head lifting back, eyes fluttering shut, as her whole being focused on the sensation searing through it.

Then he was driving into her, strong and insistent, thrusting up into her. She heard him cry out above her, felt his body explode inside hers. She cried out with him, the universe burning all around them as their bodies convulsed one within the other. It went on—a tidal wave crashing again and again through her flesh.

Her head fell back again as the final wave died away. Long moments later, he slid his hand up over her throat, his fingers curving up around the line of her jaw to cup her. Slowly, shudderingly, her pounding heart started to ease. Her panting breath to steady. She lay exhausted, shaken, as he released her, gazing blindly up at him. Shock glazed her eyes. The world returned to her, and she realised what she had done.

Had sex with a man who held her in absolute contempt.

A man whom she had more cause to hate than any man alive.

Cold drenched through her, replacing the heat of her sated body with a chill that seemed to go down to her guts, pooling into ice. Disbelief and a dismay so wrenching that it seemed to convulse her stomach choked her lungs.

Oh, God, what have I done?

Her shocked eyes could only stare upwards to the man on whose bed she was lying, whose body was still pinning her, filling her...

For an endless moment the world froze in horror. Only around the edges, like a miasma, it was haunted by the imprint of a quite, quite different emotion—an emotion that had possessed her, consumed her, enveloped her into a world she had never known existed. A world against whose loss now she heard a faint, anguished cry, as if she were losing something incredibly rare and precious, as if the loss of it were unbearable...

But filling her consciousness, spreading through it like an ugly stain, was the overpowering emotion of dismay—and shock and disbelief that she could have done what she had just done. Limp with horror at herself, she could only lie there, all limbs exhausted, staring blindly up into the face looking down at her.

For a moment there was no motion. None at all. Then abruptly, roughly, her body was away from the weight bearing on her. Nikos was striding away, across the huge room, thrusting open the door into the *en suite* bathroom, and closing it sharply behind him.

For a handful of seconds she could only lie there, still, inert, motionless. Then, forcing her frozen mind to act, she clambered up, urgently scrabbling for her clothes, forcing herself into them with unbearable haste and clumsiness, not bothering with underwear, just winding her top and her skirt around her to cover her nakedness. From the bathroom she could hear the sound of a shower starting. Her eyes flew past the door opposite the French window to the terrace, and she saw the door which surely must lead to the rest of the villa.

She hurried to it, half tripping, heart racing, lungs still choking, and yanked it open, finding herself, to her abject relief, in a service corridor. She didn't know where she was going but it didn't matter—she simply hurtled along it, desperately hoping that at this late hour she would encounter no one until she came upon part of the villa she recognised and could navigate to her own guest bedroom from there. Minutes later she was shutting the door and collapsing down on her own bed, shaking like a leaf, her arms wrapped around herself, as if stanching a wound. She started to rock.

Words whipped through her, over and over again, more and more cruel.

What have I done? What have I done?

Nikos stood beneath the pounding water of the shower. Its needles should be knives. Knives to carve into his greedy flesh the punishment he deserved.

How the hell could he have been so stupid? Hadn't he known—hadn't he told himself, staring into the mirror above the basin in that very bathroom a handful of days ago, that he was playing with fire? And now what had he gone and done? Knowingly, deliberately fooled himself on the way back to the villa with the kind of self-flattering logic that, had it been a dodgy business proposal, he'd have seen through in an instant. But which, because it was his damn male desire—never thwarted before, never not satiated, whenever and with whoever he wanted—he'd seized on it as if it were legal writ!

His mind sheered away. Sheered away from remembering the moment when he'd realised that not only did he *have* to take her, right there, right then, but worse—far, far worse— the moment when the world had simply whited out.

It's never been like that before.

The words formed in his mind as the stinging needles pounded down on him.

Never had the moment of sexual fulfilment been like that—so intense, so overpowering, so consuming that he'd cried out, unable to stop himself.

Until the moment when consciousness had knifed back into him and he'd stared down at her and realised, with harsh, pitiless self-condemnation, that he had just walked over the edge of a cliff.

Angrily his hand fisted, and he thumped it against the wall of the shower stall.

I damn well knew I should have left her alone. I damn well knew it!

But even as the words formed, so did others. Others that made him abruptly cut off the water, grab a towel, and pat himself dry, roughly towelling the moisture out of his hair. Then he cast the towels aside and yanked open the bathroom door.

He knew he should never have touched Ann Turner. He knew he should never have taken her to his bed. Knew he should never have had sex with her.

But he knew something else as well as he strode out of the bathroom.

He wanted her again.

CHAPTER SEVEN

THE SUN WAS SCARCELY UP, but Ann was lying in bed, wakeful and tormented. She would have to go. Leave Sospiris. There was no other option. She couldn't stay here now!

I'll have to think of something—something to tell Ari, Mrs Theakis. Something—anything!

Except the truth. Even as she lay there she felt a semi-hysterical bubble inside her at the thought of Mrs Theakis knowing...

She shuddered in horror, feeling her skin flush.

How am I going to face her? How can I even have breakfast with her—knowing what I did, where I was?

And yet she was going to have to. Going to have to somehow get through the morning, behave normally, then dream up some plausible reason why she had to go back to England.

A spear stabbed her. Ari! Ari would be so upset, so distressed! Wasn't it bad enough he was about to lose Tina? Now she was proposing to walk out on him as well.

For ever.

Because unless by some miracle Mrs Theakis invited her here again when Nikos was somewhere else—like Australia, or better still Antarctica!—or perhaps herself come to London some time, then how could she possibly ever see Ari again? She could never go anywhere near Nikos Theakis again—never!

Abruptly, another emotion stabbed into her. One that was shocking, unforgivable—shameless!

Never to see Nikos again—

Instantly, viciously, she slammed down on the emotion, crushing it brutally, punishingly. How could she stoop so low? How could she? And how could a man who thought her the lowest of the low, who had said such cruel, vile things about her sister, a man she had hated for four long years, have possibly made love to her the way he had?

Her face hardened. Made love? Was she stupid or something? Nikos Theakis hadn't 'made love' to her! He'd had sex with her! That was all he'd done—all he'd wanted. Bitter humiliation seared through her. Oh, how could she have fallen into bed with him like that? Just because he looked like a Greek god. Just because she felt weak at the knees because he was so devastating a male that any woman, *every* woman, would turn and stare at him and yearn for him to look their way…

Anguished, hating herself almost as much as she hated Nikos Theakis, Ann went on staring at the ceiling, counting the hours till she could escape from Sospiris. Escape from Nikos.

But what had seemed imperative as she lay sleepless and tormented on her bed became far, far more difficult when she had to face Mrs Theakis at breakfast.

'Leave us?' Sophia Theakis' eyes widened in surprise. 'Surely not?' Her gaze shifted as the doors to the morning room opened. 'Nikos! Ann is saying that she may have to return to London.'

Ann felt herself freeze. Not for all the power on earth would she turn her head to see Nikos stalk in. But nothing could stop her hearing his deep voiced reply as he took his place. 'Out of the question. It was agreed that she would stay until after Tina's wedding so that Ari would be least unsettled. Is that not so, Ann?'

Her head swivelled. And immediately, fight it as she might,

she felt colour stain vividly across her cheekbones at the sight of him. He was casually dressed in a pale cream polo shirt with a discreetly expensive logo on it, hair still damp and jaw freshly shaved. At once, vivid and hot, sprang the memory of his roughened skin against her last night as his mouth possessed hers... Her colour deepened.

His eyes were holding hers, challenging them—branding them.

She bit her lip, and saw something flare deep within. 'I—I—' she began, then floundered. Rational thought, speech, was impossible. 'It's just that—' she tried again, and failed.

Another expression shot through Nikos's eyes. She could have sworn it was satisfaction.

'Good,' he said. 'Then that is settled. You will stay, as agreed, until after Tina's wedding. And then...' His eyes flicked to her momentarily, as his hand reached for the jug of freshly squeezed orange juice in front of him. 'Then we shall see. Who knows, Ann, what will happen after Tina's wedding, hmm? In the meantime today, with Ari occupied with his playmate from Maxos arriving with Tina later this morning, it is more than time, I think, that I showed you something more of Sospiris than you have already seen.'

Calmly, he started to drink his orange juice. Numbly, Ann turned back to Mrs Theakis, as though she might somehow save her from so dire a fate. But as she turned she caught for a fleeting moment a strange, assessing look in the older woman's eyes, as they hovered between her guest and her son. Then an instant later it was gone, and Ann could only think— only hope!—she had imagined it.

Sophia Theakis' expression had changed to a serene smile. 'That is a lovely idea, Nikos. Sospiris has many hidden beauties, Ann,' she said benignly, 'and I'm sure my son will show you all of them.'

With monumental effort, Ann schooled her face into complaisance. Inside, she felt like jelly.

Nikos gunned the Jeep impatiently. Where was she? If she was planning on trying to get out of this, he would simply go and fetch her. But she would come. His mother would see to it.

For a moment his expression wavered. It was not comfortable, being under the eye of his mother in these circumstances. But it was for her sake that he was doing this—even though, of course, she could not know that. But for her to be burdened indefinitely, leached off by the female she thought so well of just because he could not open her eyes to Ann Turner's true character, was not something he was prepared to tolerate. What he *was* prepared to tolerate, however, was his own disapproval of the course of action he had decided to pursue— a course of action that he'd already taken a decision on as he'd walked back into the bedroom the night before.

To hell with it! To hell with warnings about playing with fire—it was too damn late for that. He'd not just played with fire—he'd set the bed ablaze! And it, and he, had gone up in a sheet of flame. So any warnings, any regrets, were too little, too late. If there was one thing that was now absolutely clear— had become forcibly even more crystal-clear when he'd seen his empty bed and realised that Ann had run away—it was that he was counting the hours until he could possess her again.

The remainder of his night had been a sleepless one, but not because he had been repining his seduction any more— it had been because his bed was empty, and he very definitely did not want it to be empty. He'd almost gone after her. Why she had done a runner he had no idea—unless it was to see whether he would come chasing after her. Or—a sudden frown had knitted his brow darkly—was she belatedly, seeking to assume a virtue she had just very amply demonstrated she did not have?

He brushed the thought aside. Of course Ann Turner possessed not a shred of virtue! How could she, when she had sold her own flesh and blood for cold hard cash? For a fleeting moment something jarred in his brain. The vivid memory of their union burned again in his mind. Could the woman who had so inflamed him, with whom he had cried out at the searing moment of their fulfilment—a fulfilment deeper and more intense than any he had experienced—really be the same woman whose grasping fingers had greedily closed over the cheques he had so contemptuously handed her?

And yet she was. She was that same woman. However much she inflamed him he must never forget that—not for a moment.

Certainly not now, as she finally emerged from the villa, her face set, not meeting his eyes, simply clambering up into the Jeep without a word, ignoring his hand reaching across the seat to help her in. Angry irritation flared briefly in Nikos at her obvious intention of refusing to acknowledge him. He released the handbrake, let in the clutch and sheered off, his eyes behind the sunglasses hard. He drove fast, not bothering to take the bumpy track easily, and was conscious that Ann was hanging on grimly, refusing to ask him to slow down.

He didn't stop until he slewed the Jeep to a halt at the far end of the island, down by Ari's 'secret beach'. He'd brought Ann here deliberately. Not only would they not be disturbed, but the beach hut was ideal for his purposes. It was not luxurious, but it contained the essentials—mainly a bed.

As he cut the engine, tossing his dark glasses on to the dashboard, a silence seemed to descend along with the settling cloud of white dust around the car.

He turned towards Ann. She was still sitting with one hand clutched at the doorframe, the other planted on the dash to steady herself. Her expression was stony. She was wearing, Nikos realised, exactly the same outfit she'd worn when they'd brought Ari here—beige cotton trousers and a long-

sleeved T-shirt. His eyes glinted mordantly. Did she think such a drab outfit would put him off? And why, pray, the cold shoulder? The glint came again, and there was a spark of anger in it now. 'Cold' had not been the word for her last night.

Time to stop this, right now.

'Ann,' he began, his voice edged, 'I don't know what you think you're playing at, but—'

Her head swivelled. The expression in her eyes was scorching.

'Playing at?' she threw back at him. 'I'm not *playing at* anything! I have absolutely no idea what the hell you think you're doing, but—'

He laughed. He couldn't help it. The scorching look in her eyes intensified. Absently, he noticed how it made them even more luminous.

'What I think I'm doing, Ann,' he said—and now the edge in his voice had gone, replaced by something very differerent, 'is this—'

He reached for her. Unable to help himself. He'd been wanting to do it since he'd walked into breakfast and seen her there, feeling a punch to his system that had made him want to walk right up to her and sweep her to him.

She was pliant in his arms as he drew her to him, and satisfaction surged through him as he lowered his mouth to hers. The next moment she had gone rigid—as rigid as a board— and her hands were balling against his chest, her mouth jerking away.

'Let me go! Let me—'

His mouth silenced her, catching her lips and his hand at her back slid up to hold the base of her skull, fingers spearing into her silken hair. God, she felt so good to kiss! So sweet and soft and honeyed—

Her momentary resistance had vanished, melted away into his kiss, and he took instant possession. He felt her hands

splaying out, pressing through his polo shirt against the wall of his chest.

He kissed her thoroughly, deeply—arousingly. And not just arousing her. His own body was responding as though a switch had been thrown, and desire swept through him.

Eventually, breathlessly, he surfaced, holding her still, gazing down into her eyes. They were huge.

'You were saying?' he said. The amusement was in his voice again, but different now—husky and low.

For a moment she just gazed at him blindly. Then, with a little choke, she tugged free. He let her go—he had proved his point. Handsomely.

Her face was strained. 'I don't want this.' Her voice was faint, hands knotting in her lap. 'I don't want it.'

His eyes glinted. 'Ann, no games. Not now. Last night proved that amply.' The glint intensified. 'Very amply.'

He started to reach for her again, but this time she was faster. She thrust open the Jeep door and leapt down. Nikos stared with a mix of exasperation and incredulity as she started to march back along the track. Was the girl mad? It would take a good hour to walk back to the villa, and the sun was getting high in the sky. He gave a rasp of irritation and went after her. She was only doing it as some kind of grand gesture, though heaven knew why.

He caught up with her in seconds and turned her round towards him. She was rigid, face clenched.

'Take your hands off me,' she gritted, eyes sparking. 'I told you I don't want this! What part of that don't you understand?' she bit out.

Something shifted in his eyes. 'This,' he said. Deliberately, quite deliberately, he lifted a hand to her face, letting the other one drop from her arm so that she was quite free. His eyes never leaving her, he simply drew his index finger down her cheek—lightly, like a feather.

Get FREE BOOKS and a FREE GIFT when you play the...

LAS VEGAS GAME

Just scratch off the gold box with a coin. Then check below to see the gifts you get! →

YES! I have scratched off the gold box. Please send me my **2 FREE BOOKS** and **FREE GIFT** for which I qualify. I understand that I am under no obligation to purchase any books as explained on the back of this card.

◄ DETACH AND MAIL CARD TODAY! ▼

☐ I prefer the regular-print edition
306 HDL EVNU   106 HDL EVDK

☐ I prefer the larger-print edition
376 HDL EW9D   176 HDL EW9

FIRST NAME

LAST NAME

ADDRESS

APT.#

CITY

STATE/PROV.

ZIP/POSTAL CODE

(H-P-03/09)

7	7	7	Worth TWO FREE BOOKS plus 2 FREE Gifts!
🍒	🍒	🍒	Worth TWO FREE BOOKS!
🔔	🔔	♣	TRY AGAIN!

www.eHarlequin.com

Offer limited to one per household and not valid to current subscribers of Harlequin Presents® books. All orders subject to approval.

Your Privacy - Harlequin Books is committed to protecting your privacy. Our privacy policy is available online at www.eHarlequin.com or upon request from the Harlequin Reader Service. From time to time we make our lists of customers available to reputable third parties who may have a product or service of interest to you. If you would prefer for us not to share your name and address, please check here. ☐

The Harlequin Reader Service — Here's How It Works:

BUSINESS REPLY MAIL
FIRST-CLASS MAIL   PERMIT NO. 717   BUFFALO, NY

POSTAGE WILL BE PAID BY ADDRESSEE

HARLEQUIN READER SERVICE
3010 WALDEN AVE
PO BOX 1867
BUFFALO NY 14240-9952

NO POSTAGE
NECESSARY
IF MAILED
IN THE
UNITED STATES

He saw her eyes flicker, saw her pupils dilate. Then he let his hand fall.

She didn't turn, or run, or march away. She simply stood there, on the track, the sun pouring down on her pale hair, swaying slightly. There was a helpless look on her face.

'That's the part I don't understand, Ann,' he said, his voice low. 'The part where I only have to touch you and you respond to me. Or not even touch you…'

His gaze held hers, lambent with desire for her. 'Do you think I haven't wanted you from when I first saw how beautiful you had become? All that was required was—opportunity.' His hand lifted to her face again. This time he slid his fingers around her jaw, feathering her hair, his thumb playing with the tender lobe of her ear. She did not move. Very slowly, her eyelashes lowered over her eyes. His other hand lifted, his thumb going to her lips, tracing across their fullness. Then, as she still stood there motionless, eyes shut in the silence all around, he gently pressed down on her lower lip with the pad of his thumb, even as his mouth came down sensuously, languorously, to take its place.

He felt her give. Felt her mouth slowly start to move against his. Felt the stiffness leave her body, the rigidity ease, dissolve. She was dissolving against him. She was exploring, tasting every moment of the sweet, delectable arousing. How long he kissed her, standing as they were alone, at the edge of the deserted beach, he did not know. Only knew that at some point he let his mouth ease from hers, felt his hand slip into hers, take it lightly, loosely, but enough to lead her, as if she were still in a daze, towards the little stone building. She came willingly, unresistingly.

Just as he had known she would.

Light filtered through the wooden shutters. It slanted narrow fingers across the bed, casting planes of dark and shade across the strong face lying so close to Ann's. She lay looking at it a moment. The eyes were shut and the features in repose. He looked—replete. The word came to her, and she knew it was apt. For herself she was—drained. Drained of everything— all emotion, all will. She could only go on lying there, her naked body held slackly against his. Her mind was a miasma, floating adrift in a strange state. She'd gone, she knew, beyond conscious thought—because what *could* she think? What was it possible to think, rationally, about what she had done? What was happening? It wasn't possible, that was all.

It was barely sane…

Because how could it be sane to sink again into the bliss she had known last night when that bliss came courtesy of a man who made his contempt of her no secret? And yet that man, that harsh, condemning man, so sneeringly offering her money for Ari, for her time here on Sospiris, seemed a universe away from the man who had initiated her into an ecstasy she had never known existed…

She felt something squeeze inside her that was almost pain. *But it's the same man…* The whisper formed in her head, and she felt that strange, squeezing pain again.

Her eyes shadowed. *Is it the same man—is it?*

Her head told her yes, but her body—oh, her body denied it with all its power.

Without conscious thought, she let her hand press against his warm, hard body, smoothed the golden skin. He was so beautiful to touch. She felt her heart give that little squeeze again, felt a strange catch in her breath, as if in wonder—in homage—at such perfection.

The long lashes lifted from his eyes, and immediately his gaze focussed on her. Equally immediately she felt as if those incredible dark eyes were piercing right into her. She felt naked—

'Ann—'

It was all he said, but it was said in a voice that sounded

as replete as he was. He glided the hand resting on her upper arm along its smooth surface. It was not sexual, not arousing. It was just because she was there. In his bed. Beside him.

'Ann,' he said again, and drew her more closely against him, settling himself into the bedding, feeling her slender body curved against his. It felt good—but then everything about her felt good. Idly, he went on smoothing his palm along her upper arm. He felt full, at rest. And after a while he started to caress her again.

This time arousingly.

And yet again Ann went with him where he wanted to go.

The Jeep was rattling over the trackway again, heading back to the villa. Nikos was driving a lot more sedately now—and why not? His ill-tempered mood of the outward journey had disappeared completely. Of course it had! Ann's ludicrous and incomprehensible show of resistance had taken him nothing more than a few moments to dispose of. Why she'd done it he had no idea, and he didn't much care. It had obviously been some kind of ploy, and it had equally obviously been completely pointless. Anyway, it was irrelevant now. All that mattered was that it was over and would not be returning.

A smile played around his mouth. No, Ann had proved—conclusively and incontrovertibly—that she was completely incapable of resisting him. Which was exactly what he'd known all along.

Just as he'd known—the smile around his mouth deepened—that his decision to stick to the strategy of making Ann Turner his mistress was the right one. Every cell in his body told him blatantly that it was certainly the right one for him personally.

As his mistress, Ann Turner was malleable, enjoyable—definitely enjoyable!—and above all disposable. His strategy was foolproof. He'd been mad to think it had any risk to it.

Not only was he now going to be able to stop Ann Turner from being a thorn in his flesh, but her own exquisite flesh was his to enjoy—to enjoy with an intensity that had proved as real today as it had last night. Just why there was such an extraordinary intensity he didn't much care—he wasn't about to question it, just make the most of it.

Whenever he could.

His smile faded, replaced by a tightening of his mouth. Now, that was going to be an impediment he didn't welcome. But it would have to be managed, all the same, until he could take Ann back to Athens with him.

He turned his head to speak to her.

'We're going to have to be discreet, you understand? But I will see what can be done to make time for you.'

A looming hairpin bend made him look back at the road. Then, having negotiated it, he said, having got no response to his comment, 'Ann?'

He glanced at her again. She appeared not to have heard him.

'Ann?' he said again, now with a slight edge in his voice.

'Yes, I heard you. Thank you,' she answered.

Nikos considered her profile. Was she put out because he'd said they would need to be discreet? Perhaps she didn't understand that there was no way he was going to expose his mother to what they were doing? Or perhaps she thought he was not intending to continue with her—or that the necessity for discretion was in fact a lack of appreciation for her on his part? Well, that could easily be sorted—no problem. He knew exactly what would keep her sweet.

And it wasn't just sex…

Ann sat on her bed, the shutters of her bedroom window drawn, locking out the light of the day. Locking out the world. She had told a maid she'd passed on her way in that she had a migraine and would be keeping to her room.

Blankness enveloped her. She knew with one part of her mind that it was a kind of safety mechanism, like anaesthesia, blocking everything else out. The blankness made her calm—very calm. In a little while, but not just now, she would think about what she had to do. But not just yet. Not quite yet. Soon.

She ought to go down and see Ari. After all, that was why she was here. But she couldn't face it. She needed time—time here on her own, with the world locked out, safe.

Safe from Nikos.

But she wasn't safe from him. She had proved that, conclusively and indelibly. He only had to touch her and she was lost.

And there was no point bewailing it, no point being angry with herself, feeling ashamed. She had tried to resist him, tried to reject him, and failed. Failed completely.

How could any woman say no to Nikos Theakis when he wanted her?

But somehow, cost what it would, she was going to have to find the strength to do just that.

A bleak look crossed her eyes.

She couldn't cope. That was the only thing she knew about this whole situation.

But why? That was the question that wrung her mind. Why?

Why had Nikos Theakis seduced her?

It didn't make sense. He could have his pick of women—women from his own world—so why bother with her, a woman he openly despised? Surely not just to prove to her that he could? He hadn't liked her attempt to reject him—was that it? His male ego demanded her submission to him? Was that all it was? He wanted her to be as susceptible to him as every other woman must surely be?

Well, she thought heavily, he had all the proof he needed of that now! His ego could rest easy—she could no more say no to him than honey could refuse to melt over a hot spoon!

Restlessly, she got to her feet, starting to pace around the room. The blankness was leaving her now, and she wished it wasn't. It was like anaesthesia wearing off…

With every portion of her body she could feel the physical evidence of what she had done—her muscles were stretched, her lips beestung, and between her thighs a low throbbing beat to her pulse. She headed for the bathroom. A shower would help, surely? And it would give her something to do—something other than letting impossible thoughts go round and round in her head, like rats in a trap.

When she emerged from the shower they were still going round, but they no longer mattered. How could it matter that she did not know why Nikos Theakis was so determined to prove her vulnerability to him? How could it matter that he only had to touch her for her to melt into his caress?

Because from now on it wasn't going to happen. From now on, even if she had to lie and be evasive, say whatever it took, she would not spend one minute alone with Nikos. Not a single minute.

She dared not.

She knew it was cowardice, but so what? If that was what was necessary to keep her safe, but still with Ari, then so be it. It would be hard, but so what? If she could just hold to her line then she would be safe. There was nothing Nikos could do to her if she refused ever to be alone with him.

It was either that or leaving Sospiris. And she wouldn't be chased off by him! She *wouldn't!* This was her only opportunity to see her nephew, her sister's son, and nothing would make her give that up!

Resolution filled her. She was here for Ari—that was all, and that was what she must remember. Nothing else.

She kept her mind focussed on that resolution as, deliberately trying to divert her mind from the tormenting channels it was running in so fixedly, she occupied herself in catching up with her correspondence—including the large number of postcards she had bought on Maxos. Writing them did her good—it reminded her of the world far beyond Sospiris, touching essential base with her real life.

She ought to go down for nursery tea, she knew, but she was too chary of Tina's astute eyes. Surely it must be branded across her forehead just what she had gone and done? No, Ari had his playmate. He would not notice his aunt's absence particularly, and she had already said she had a migraine. She had better make the most of it and keep to her room. Hiding.

She knew that was what she was doing but she needed to do it. Strengthen her resolve. Prepare her mental barriers.

And pray they would hold.

Nikos strolled along the corridor, his mood enjoyably anticipatory. It had been annoying to discover, on emerging from his office for his mother's pre-prandial drinks, that Ann was apparently in her room with a migraine, and was not coming down to dinner. Damn—evidently Ann had indeed understood the need for discretion. If he'd only known sooner she was in her room, and not with Ari, he could easily have slipped along there at some point. He'd had to endure a dinner without her that had seemed to go on for ever until now, pleading some late night work he had to attend to, he could head straight for Ann's room.

Outside her door, he knocked briefly, then walked in. Already he was eager for her—the beach chalet seemed far too long ago.

His eyes went to her immediately. She was in bed waiting for him, idly flicking through an English language magazine.

'*Kalispera,* Ann,' he said, as he walked into the room.

The magazine dropped as if it were a hot stone, and her head snapped up. Shock emptied her face. He strolled across the room and sat down on the bed.

'I'm sorry you've had to wait for me—I only learnt at

dinner that you were keeping to your room. I'd been working till then. My apologies.' He leant forward, unable to resist the pleasure of making skin contact, drawing the back of his hand down her cheek.

She jerked, as if an electric shock had gone through her. Nikos smiled. That was good. Responsive.

Just the way he wanted her.

Then, as if his touch had thrown a switch, she spoke.

'What the hell do you think you're doing here?' Her voice was half a croak, half a whisper.

He gave a low laugh. 'Don't panic. I've been very discreet, the way I told you we would need to be.'

'*Discreet.*' She said the word as if it were an expletive.

He gave a shrug. 'It's inconvenient, yes, but there it is. My mother has certain codes of behaviour, and I would not wish to breach them openly.'

Even as he spoke he was conscious of a sense of discomfort. He did not relish this aspect of the business—but it was for his mother's sake in the long run that he made Ann Turner his mistress and got her greedy claws out of the Theakis family by putting her beyond the pale of his mother's misplaced forbearance of her.

'Inconvenient—' Her voice was hollow now, and she was staring at him with a peculiar expression in her face.

'Ann,' he said, making his tone temporising, 'for the time being it's unavoidable. But as soon as Tina's wedding is over I'll take you to Athens and—'

'Take me to Athens?' Her voice had changed to incomprehension.

It started to irritate Nikos. Why did she have to repeat everything he said to her?

'Well, Athens first, and then wherever you'd like to go—though of course I'd have to fit any vacation around my obligations to business, alas. But all the same—'

He never finished his sentence.

Her face snapped shut. Like a door closing. Shutting him out. Very decidedly out.

'I,' she bit out, and her eyes were hard suddenly—like stones, 'am not going *anywhere* with you. I am *not*—' she made the emphasis as if it was a razor slicing down '—going to have some hole and corner affair with you! Get out—get out of my room, right now!'

His eyes flashed impatiently. 'Ann—enough. We've been through this little farce once already today. I don't appreciate games—especially when they've already been played out. It's going to be difficult enough as it is, finding time together, without you doing your pointless denial routine. So—'

He didn't get any further. She was scrambling out of bed, the other side from him. Immediately Nikos's eyes went to her body, its slender form outlined beneath the diaphanous nightgown by the lamp from her bedside, to the tender mounds of her breasts, the slender wand of her waist and the graceful swell of her hips with the darkened vee between the perfect column of her thighs, all barely veiled by the translucent fabric. He felt himself respond—*Theos*, she was so beautiful! Desire surged through him. He wanted her—was hungry for her, could not wait for her.

'Ann—' Her name came, husked, raw. He started to move, levering off the bed, heading round its foot towards her, to reach her, touch her, to fold her to him, feel that beautiful, arousing body in his arms, that sweet, honeyed mouth opening to his...

And then, to his disbelief, even as his eyes devoured her she gave a little cry and hurled herself into the *en suite* bathroom. Nikos heard the frantic turning of the key in the lock, and then there was silence. For a long, incredulous moment he could only stare at the locked door.

Anger surged through him. Anger, disbelief—and intense, obliterating frustration.

Then, like a zombie, he walked out of the room.

Still not believing what had just happened.

CHAPTER EIGHT

'OH, ARI, THAT'S *very* good. Well done!'

Ann was on the terrace outside the nursery, shaded from the sun by an awning. Ari was colouring a drawing of his beloved trains.

'Why not write their names under the picture?' said Ann. She started to write a dotted outline that Ari could use to trace the shapes of the letters. Tina looked up from where she was checking off 'Things to do' for her wedding.

'You know about children, don't you? Using dots for letters?' she observed.

Ann smiled. 'It's a good way to get them to control the shape, I think.' She watched attentively as Ari started to write. It was good to be here with him. Good to be with the lively little boy who was the whole purpose of her presence here at the Theakis villa. The *sole* purpose.

A purpose which did *not* include providing on-tap sex for Nikos Theakis whenever he felt like waltzing into her bedroom! No, she mustn't remember that—and she mustn't let in, not even by a hair's breadth, the emotions that went with the memory. She must just shut it out. Ruthlessly. With an impermeable seal.

Nikos had used the term 'denial' and she clung to it. Yes, denial was exactly what she had to do. Deny everything. Deny she had ever felt such insane weakness for the man. Deny she could still, if for a moment she allowed it, feel the haunting echo of his touch, his caresses, his intoxicating invasion…possession.

Her eyes hardened. Possession. Yes, that was a good word. As in helping himself to her. Just because she was convenient—handy. Deliberately she let her hackles bristle. Nikos Theakis was a man so arrogant that he actually thought he could just help himself to sex with her! It didn't even bother him that he held her in total contempt for having taken his money from him! A chilling thought went through her. Was it because of what he thought of her that he also thought he could just help himself to her body? Was it because he held her in such contempt that he saw no problem with casually seducing her?

A shadow seemed to fall across her, making her shiver inwardly. To be held in such contempt that he thought he could use her sexually for his fleeting convenience…

'Kyria Ann?'

She surfaced from her dark cogitations to find one of the maids hovering.

'Please come…' said the girl in hesitant English.

Wondering why, but getting to her feet all the same, nodding to Tina and murmuring to Ari that she would be back soon, Ann followed the maid back indoors. Did Mrs Theakis want to see her? But the room she was shown into was not Sophia Theakis' sitting room.

It was Nikos Theakis's office. And seated at the desk, the flickering computer screen to his side, his planed face illuminated through the half-closed slats of the Venetian blinds at the window, was Nikos.

Too late she made the realisation as she stepped inside. The maid closed the door behind her. Too late she instantly turned to leave.

'Don't bolt, Ann. I have something to say to you. Sit down.'

The voice was clipped and impersonal.

She looked across at him. He was formally dressed in a business suit. She hadn't seen him so formal since they had arrived. And she had forgotten just how formidable he could look—every inch the captain of industry, born to give orders and have them obeyed by a host of minions doing his bidding.

Well, she wasn't one of them! Automatically she felt her hackles rise, and she stiffened.

'There's nothing I want to hear from you,' she said tersely.

Something flickered in his darkly veiled eyes, and she felt a shimmer go through her.

He did not reply, instead sliding open a drawer in the desk and removing an object. It was long and slim. He placed it at the front of the desk, facing her.

'This, Ann,' he said, and his eyes did not change expression, 'is yours.'

Warily, as if it might be a loaded gun, she reached for it. What was it? And why was Nikos telling her it was hers? She picked it up and realised that it was a case of some kind. It could be a case for spectacles, or a pen. But why should that make it hers?

She opened the case.

And stared disbelievingly.

A ribbon of white fire glittered in the dim light.

'What is this?' Ann heard her own voice speaking.

'A diamond necklace. Whilst I appreciate you prefer to operate on a cash basis, that is not something I am prepared to do in these circumstances. But you are welcome to see the receipt for the necklace—to know how much I consider you are worth. You can be flattered, Ann—it's a considerable amount.'

She dragged her eyes from the necklace, glittering against the dark velvet of the interior of the jewel case. She looked at him. There was a glitter in his eyes too, as if reflecting the diamonds he was offering her. She felt an emotion spear through her. She did not know its name—only that it was powerful. Very powerful.

'You see...' said Nikos, and he shifted very slightly in his seat, the hand that was resting on the polished mahogany surface of his desk flexing minutely. His eyes with that dark glitter were still resting on her. 'I have decided to cut to the chase. As a businessman I apply the motivations that are sufficient for each transaction to succeed. Your motivation, Ann, is consistent—money. Money is what drives your actions— whether it is giving up your sister's child, or giving up your invaluable time to come to Sospiris. And therefore I apply it now to this transaction—albeit in a form that is, let us say, an alternative to cash. So—' he took a sharp intake of breath '—now that we have successfully concluded this transaction, you must excuse me. I am leaving for Athens shortly. But I will be back later tonight. Wear the necklace when I come to you, Ann.' He paused, and the dark glitter intensified. 'Just the necklace.'

She went on standing there, immobile, incapable of moving, incapable of anything except feeling the emotion spearing through her. Then, from somewhere, she found her voice.

'You think a diamond necklace will get you into my bed?'

She said it flatly, getting the words out past the emotion that was seizing on them even as she spoke them.

'Why not? Your track record shows you are very amenable to such an approach to life.' There was a twist to his mouth as he answered her, his voice terse.

It made the emotion spear deeper into her. Her eyes went to the necklace again—the necklace Nikos was offering her in exchange for sex. Emotion bit again—a different one. One that seemed to touch the very quick of her. But she must not allow that emotion—only the other one, which was as sharp as the point of a spear.

Her eyes pulled away, back to the man sitting in his handmade suit at his antique desk, rich and powerful and arrogant. The man who had kissed her deeply, caressed the intimacies of her body, who had melded his body with hers, who had transported her to an ecstasy she had never known existed.

Who was offering her a diamond necklace for sex...

Carefully, very carefully, she snapped shut the lid of the box and placed it back in front of him.

'I am not,' she said, 'a whore.'

His expression did not change. 'Your sister,' he said softly—so softly that it raised the hairs on the back of her neck— 'possessed at least one virtue. She did not try and disguise the truth about herself. But you, Ann—you are a hypocrite. Worse even than your sister. Your sister sold her body—you, you sold your own flesh and blood. You sold her child.' His gaze seared her. 'So do not stand there and attempt to look *virtuous* or *insulted*—' each word dripped from him with acid contempt '—because I'm offering you what your sister was happy enough to take from any man she could persuade to make a similar offer!'

Like a floodgate breaking, emotion surged in Ann. Powerful and overpowering.

'Don't speak of Carla like that! And take your diamonds and *choke* on them!'

She whirled around, blind with fury.

How she got out of there she didn't know, but the moment she was in the corridor all she could do was stand there, shaking. Then, looking wildly around her, she plunged through the villa until she found her own bedroom, and there, safe in its sanctuary, she threw herself down on her bed.

Hot, hard tears convulsed in her throat. Fevered and furious. Choking her as they racked her. Face down on her pillow she cried tears for Carla, dead in her grave, whom even death could not save from the vile insults of Nikos Theakis—

a man who could take a woman to ecstasy, a paradise of the senses, and yet think her nothing more than a whore...

It was like acid poured on a wound, burning and biting into raw flesh.

She fisted her hands, pushing herself up on her elbows, neck straining, staring at the headboard, tears staining her cheeks.

Why—*why* should she be reacting like this? She'd known Nikos despised her for what she had done—and she had already castigated herself for succumbing to a man who could still take a woman to bed that he thought so contemptuously of.

And yet this was different. Offering her a diamond necklace, in exchange for her body. Expecting her to accept it.

And why? Because it brought home to her the brutal reality of it—that was all she was to Nikos Theakis. Nothing more.

Rage, convulsing and blinding, shook through her. But beneath the rage was another emotion. The one she had felt reach the very quick of her. The one that brought not fury but something quite different. That made her want to curl up into a ball and clasp her arms around her, as if to stanch a wound.

A wound that had gone much, much deeper than should ever be possible.

Nikos sat at his desk. He hadn't moved a muscle since she'd gone storming out of his office.

Without the diamond necklace.

He shifted his eyes so they rested on the jewel case.

Why hadn't she taken it?

It didn't make sense.. Everything he knew about her—everything she had proved to him—had told him that she would snatch the necklace from his hand as eagerly as she'd taken his cheques.

Even more eagerly.

The expression in his eyes changed minutely. After all, it was not as if she had found being in his bed repulsive...

But it was a mistake to admit any thoughts about Ann Turner in his bed. Immediately, hungrily, appetite leapt within him. It had been twenty-four long, deprived hours since he had taken her to the beach chalet, and his body was protesting the absence of a repeat encounter. It had protested quite enough last night, when he had been left unsatisfied, thwarted. But then at least he had had the prospect of remedying the situation by dint of the means he'd just put into play.

Cutting to the chase had been exactly what he'd intended. No more prevaricating, manipulating games from Ann Turner. Just cutting to the chase and giving her exactly what she was so obviously angling for—what was so obviously the reason behind all her ploys of denial and evasion. Because what other reason could there be for her evasion of him? Her denial of her response to him? He only had to touch her for her to light up like a flame—and, *Theos mou,* it was the same for him! One touch from her and he wanted her instantly—totally.

The way he did right now.

He shifted restlessly, his thoughts biting with a poisonous mix of frustration and incomprehension.

Why had she refused the necklace? What did she think she was going to achieve by refusing it?

His mouth thinned. Well, there was one thing she was going to achieve, that was for sure.

He seized up the house phone. As Yannis answered, Nikos barked down it, 'Phone Kyria Constantis and inform her that she is invited to dine here tonight.' Then he put the receiver down. He glowered darkly into the space in front of the desk, where Ann Turner had refused to take the necklace.

So she didn't want the necklace, and she didn't want him. His mouth tightened even more. There were plenty of women who *did* want him. And tonight Ann Turner would get an eyeful of one of them.

CHAPTER NINE

ELENA CONSTANTIS WAS speaking Greek, clearly intent on cutting out Ann and Tina. Ann was glad of it. Glad that she could focus her whole attention on Tina, discussing her forthcoming wedding, and give none at all—not the slightest iota—to the man to whom Elena Constantis was devoting *her* attention at the dinner table.

She was welcome to him.

Every woman on God's earth was welcome to him.

Emotions still roiled within her like bilge water—dark and angry. She had got through the remainder of the day somehow, but she wasn't even sure how. She'd had to stay in her room until she could finally face going back downstairs, face washed, breathing controlled. But it had still been hard. Hard to behave normally, and harder still now, in Nikos's loathsome presence at dinner.

Abruptly, Elena switched back to English—and to Ann.

'Will you be looking after darling little Ari as his new nanny?' she enquired in saccharine tones.

'I am his aunt, but I'm only visiting, Kyria Constantis,' replied Ann. 'I have no qualifications to be a professional nanny.'

The Greek woman's eyes hardened a moment. 'Yes, even on a salary as generous as working for a family such as the Theakises would bring you, it would be difficult to afford

designer clothes,' she purred. Her heavily mascaraed eyes
flicked over Ann's dress, then became tinged with satisfaction. 'I do love your outfit—I had one very similar when that
particular collection came out. When was it now? Oh, five
years ago, I believe. It has scarcely dated at all!'

'Yes,' responded Ann, not rising to the pinprick. 'Some
fashions last longer than others.'

Longer than those who bought them—

The unbidden thought rose in her mind, making her throat
tighten suddenly and her vision blur. Emotionally raw as she
was, despite her outward display of calm, as she blinked to
clear her eyes she diverted her thoughts from their painful
subject and became aware of Nikos Theakis' dark gaze resting
on her. Or rather on her dress. He was staring at it critically.

Ann's mouth thinned. *Oh, yes, go on, do,* she thought viciously. *Cost it down to the last penny—something to
condemn me for!* Why should she care what he thought of her?

*I won't let myself be hurt by what he did today! I won't! I
knew all along that he despised me for taking his money, and
I knew it was just sex that he wanted me for! Just sex—a
passing appetite. He helped himself, and didn't have to think
twice about it, because he thought he only had to toss me a
diamond necklace and I'd roll over for him! Because that's
the sort of woman he thinks I am.*

So how can a man like that hurt me?

A silent shudder went through her. Thank God she had the
strength to know she must not have anything more to do with
Nikos Theakis! Had had that strength even when he was
sitting on her very bed, reaching for her, and her whole body
was suddenly aflame. Because if she hadn't, if she had
allowed Nikos to sweep away her frail, pathetic defences
against him, as he had done on the beach she would never have
known just how low he thought her.

But now she did. Bald, brutal knowledge. And she had to

cling on to it with all her might. Like clutching a scorpion to her breast.

Somehow she got through the rest of the meal. But that night, as she lay in her bed in the beautiful guest bedroom, despite all the luxury of the Theakis villa around her she felt very alone.

Nikos would not be alone, she knew, with a tearing feeling inside her that she knew she must not, *must* not feel. No, tonight he would have Elena to keep him company! It would be Elena who would know the sensual bliss of his touch, the lush pleasure of his kisses, his caressing. Her body which would catch fire, burn in the flames he would arouse—her throat that would cry out at the moment of consummation, of ecstasy.

The pang came again, like a stiletto blade sliding between her ribs, seeking the quick of her flesh. Restlessly she turned over, pulling the bed coverings around her, wanting only the oblivion of sleep.

When it came, it brought no peace. Only the torment of dreams—dreams she would have given a diamond necklace *not* to have! And it brought too—dimly, like an excess thudding of her heart—a sound penetrating her unconsciousness that she did not quite believe: the thudding of helicopter rotors.

But in the morning she discovered that the Theakis helicopter had indeed been busy. Not only had it ferried Elena Constantis back to Maxos just after midnight, but it had also just departed again, this time taking Nikos with it.

'He must spend some time in the office, he tells me,' said Mrs Theakis to Ann over breakfast. 'He will be back for Tina's wedding, of course. Now, my dear,' she went on, 'how are you feeling this morning?'

She gave her customary serene smile, but even as Ann managed to murmur politely that she felt better, thank you, simultaneously trying not to show the relief on her face at hearing that Nikos had left Sospiris, she was sure she saw an assessing flicker in her hostess's expression. Then it was gone.

For the next few days Ann devoted herself entirely to Ari, glad to do so. But if during the day she told herself—over and over again—how glad she was too for the respite from Nikos's presence, at night her unconscious mind was a traitor to her, giving back in dreams what was a treacherous torment, a coruscating humiliation to remember. The sensual bliss she had felt in his arms. She awoke restless, aching, yet knowing she must not, *must not* feel that way…

And not just her unconscious mind was traitor to her. For when, the day before Tina's family were due to arrive for the forthcoming wedding, Ann came down to dinner, she discovered Nikos had returned to Sospiris.

She was taken by surprise—she had thought she had another twenty-four hours to steel herself. But she had no time at all—none. And that—surely only that?—must be why she felt her heart crunch in her chest. Just shock and being unprepared. That was all. Not because her eyes went to him immediately and her stomach hollowed, as she took in his tall, commanding figure, sheathed in that hand-made business suit of his, with a dark silk tie echoing the raven satin of his hair, the planed face, the sculpted mouth, the hooded long-lashed eyes that flicked devastatingly to her.

She felt them scorch her, as if a laser had gone through her, and in them was something that made her breath catch.

No! Her own weakness appalled her. God, she'd had days to collect herself, compose herself.

Cure herself.

Because cure herself she must. No other possibility was acceptable. She had to cure herself so that she could look at Nikos Theakis and see him as Tina saw him—as nothing more than a ridiculously handsome male who could turn female heads for miles around, but not hers. Her he left cold—quite, quite cold.

Except that *cold* was not the sensation flushing through her now. Not in the slightest.

It was heat beating up through her, invading her skin, her body cells, her mind, her brain.

Taking her over.

'Ah, Ann, my dear—there you are.' As ever, it was Sophia Theakis' placid voice that made her surface, made her brain work again, made her drag her eyes from the man who had magnetised them with his presence.

Another presence helped distract her as well. A little figure came running across to her.

'Uncle Nikki is back! And Dr Sam is coming too! And I am staying up, and I am *not* going to fall asleep and go splat into my dinner, like Uncle Nikki says!'

Ann stooped to catch up Ari and return his hug. His presence at dinner was a godsend, and so was Sam's. He arrived shortly, escorted in by Tina, who was looking very fetching in a blush-pink dress that suited her dusky curls. They made a striking couple, and Ann felt a strange pang go through her as they stood together, so obviously a pair, Tina's hand hooked into Sam's arm, and their shoulders brushing.

Lucky Tina, came the thought again. But she put it aside, knowing she had to focus only on getting through this meal without looking anywhere near Nikos.

Somehow she did, and it was mostly thanks to Ari, who held centre stage, having both his uncle and a clearly amused Sam to entertain with his chatter. As the lengthy meal drew to a close, however, despite his assurance that he would not fall asleep, Ann could see Ari getting sleepier and sleepier. It gave her just the opportunity she needed to murmur to Tina that she should stay with Sam while she put Ari to bed. Scooping up the nearly somnolent infant, she bore him off, smiling her goodnights to everyone round the table except the man at the head of it. He, with her blessing, could fall off a cliff for all she cared.

At least, she thought darkly, Nikos was ignoring her as

much as she was ignoring him. And with Tina's parents and immediate family arriving the next day, surely there should be people enough to make it possible for her to go on avoiding him?

But her hopes were dashed the very next morning.

'My dear,' said Mrs Theakis to her during breakfast, at which Ann was doing her best to continue her policy of ignoring Nikos, even though his presence was about as easy to ignore as a jackal's at a watering hole. 'It would afford me a great pleasure to be allowed to make you a present of a new gown to wear for Tina's wedding reception evening party.'

Immediately Ann demurred. 'Oh, no, really—it's very kind of you, but I brought an evening gown with me, just in case.'

Mrs Theakis gave an airy wave of her beringed hand. 'I am sure that a new one would be far more fun for you.' She smiled.

'No—really. The one I have is fine, I promise you,' insisted Ann. Not only did she *not* want Ari's grandmother spending money on her, she was also painfully conscious of what would obviously be Nikos's caustic disapproval of her getting yet more out of the Theakis family.

The next moment she was even more grateful that she had refused.

'Nikos is going to Athens today—he could take you with him and help you choose a new dress,' said Mrs Theakis encouragingly.

Ann's expression was a study. 'No—please—really,' she stammered out.

To her intense relief Mrs Theakis dropped the subject, but as Ann headed back to her room after breakfast to brush her teeth, she was intercepted at her bedroom door.

'Show me this dress of yours,' said a brusque, terse voice behind her. She turned sharply. Nikos was bearing down on her. 'My mother is clearly too tactful to say that she would like you to wear something appropriate for Tina's reception. If I can't reassure her, then—like it or not—I'll have to let her splash out on a new one for you,' he said, with evident disapproval.

Ann's eyes snapped. 'It's a perfectly respectable evening gown, thank you very much!'

'I'll be the judge of that,' said Nikos darkly, and pushed past her into the room.

It was hard to see him there again, dominating the space as he dominated every space. He had not been inside since the night he'd walked in for a bit of sex on the side...

The last thing she wanted was to see him there again, but if it meant that she could evade the unthinkable prospect of going to Athens with him to buy a new dress she would endure it. Stiffly, Ann marched to the wardrobe and leafed through her clothes, taking out the evening gown she had brought with her from London. It was a beautiful gown—in deep turquoise layered chiffon, with one shoulder bare and the other a broad pleat of material. The bodice was a little too low cut for her liking, but she had made a tuck in the shoulder strap to hoist the bodice higher, reducing her décolletage. Originally, too, the long skirt had been split to the thigh, but Ann had painstakingly sewn up the two sections to make it much less revealing.

A sudden oath sounded behind her, startling her. Before she could stop him, Nikos had snatched the dress from her.

'Where did you get this?' he snarled.

Ann looked askance at his incomprehensible anger. Then, before she could gather an answer, he provided one himself.

'Don't bother to answer with a lie! I recognised it immediately!' His voice was harsh and grating. 'Your sister wore it the night she got her avaricious claws into my brother!'

Ann could only stare. Shock and fury etched her face. Anger flashed again in Nikos' eyes. He threw the dress to the floor, and Ann, giving a little cry, made an instinctive movement to pick it up from where it lay crumpled in a heap. But hard hands came around her elbows, pinning her immobile.

'Were you planning it deliberately?' The snarl was in his voice, in his contorted face. 'Flaunting that dress in front of me—in front of my mother!'

Ann's face worked. 'I didn't have the faintest idea of—'

He thrust her away. 'No? Then why choose to bring it here?' he demanded.

'Because it's a beautiful dress, that's all!' she answered agitatedly. 'I didn't know—' She took a heavy, ragged breath. 'I didn't know you'd recognise it….'

Her mind raced on. How had he recognised it at all? How on earth should *he* know what dress her sister had been wearing when she'd met his brother?

A sound came from his throat. It was one of revulsion.

'Oh, I would recognise that dress, all right.' His voice was like a razorblade. Dark eyes bored into hers. 'It's indelibly etched on my memory.' The razor scraped across her flesh. 'Especially when your sister was taking it off in front of me…'

Ann stared. There was ice forming in her stomach.

Nikos's eyes were dark. Black, like pits. He started to speak.

'Andreas and I were guests on a yacht, cruising off Monte Carlo. The owner—a business associate we were currently in negotiation with—was the kind of man who liked to have a lot of girls on tap for any guests who might not have brought their own partners for the occasion. I don't have to tell you what kind of girls they were, do I?' His voice was mordant, his eyes still boring into hers. 'The kind that like to party at other people's expense. But let us say they pay for their passage in their own way…'

A breath was raked into him. 'Your sister targeted me right from the outset. Girls like her are amateurs only in name— she had done her research. She knew exactly who I was, how much I was worth, and that on that occasion I had no female partner with me. Her mistake, however—' his voice twisted

'—was in thinking I would have any interest in a girl like her. My indifference didn't put her off, though—she took it as a personal challenge.' His lips curled. 'On the last night, as we headed back to Monaco, I went back to my cabin and she was there, waiting for me. Wearing that dress.'

His eyes flicked to the vivid heap of material on the floor. Then they whipped back to Ann. His voice dropped to Arctic.

'She came on to me, stripping the dress off her body, determined to seduce me—determined to get into my bed and get the reward she wanted for it. When I turned her down, telling her to get dressed and get out, she spat at me that she'd make me sorry. I threw her out and thought I'd done with her. The next day—' his expression was like granite '—I woke to discover she'd taken off with Andreas.'

His eyes narrowed to slits as he iced his words at Ann. 'Your bitch of a sister helped herself to *my brother* out of spite. Because I refused to take her as my mistress and drape her in the diamonds she sold her body for!'

As his ugly words fell into the silence between them Ann felt sick. Through the agonising tightness in her throat, she forced herself to speak.

'She cared for Andreas—I know she did. I saw them together.'

'She cared for his money, that was all. The Theakis wealth. That's what she got pregnant for.'

His stark, cruel denunciation stabbed as punishingly as it had done four years ago, when Nikos Theakis had come to take Ari from her. She looked away, down at the crumpled dress on the floor. Slowly she bent to pick it up. She couldn't wear it now. She stared at it a moment. Then she turned back to Nikos. His face was still stark.

Was that really what Carla had done—tried to get Nikos to make her his mistress, and then turned to Andreas out of spite when she was rejected?

It was horrible to think of—horrible to think of the world Carla had lived in—a world where she had been regarded as some toy by rich men, as one of any number of girls provided for entertainment. Paying her way on a luxury yacht by making herself sexually available, out to get what she could, any way she could, from the rich men there...

I never wanted to think about Carla like that. It was always too horrible—too sordid. But that's the way Nikos saw her—with his own eyes...

Sombrely she put the dress away, smoothing down its folds. 'I won't wear it,' she said in a low voice.

But words grated from him. 'No—wear it, Ann. Wear it and look in the mirror when you do. And see the woman you are. Like your sister—beautiful on the outside, but on the inside—'

He stopped, mouth tightening. For a moment his eyes burned into hers, and she felt slain by them. Then, without another word, he walked from her room.

Her thoughts that day remained sombre, disturbed. Nikos had ripped a veil from her—a veil she had kept in place of her own volition. She had known what was beneath, but had not wanted to look. But it was there, all the same. Indelible. Staining her sister's memory.

No wonder he hated her so much.

The words formed in her mind, weaving in and out of her thoughts, haunting her. She tried not to hear them, but they would not leave her.

She did her best, though—busying herself first with Ari, who was getting progressively more excited as the day went on, then with greeting Tina's family, and then with the enlarged company for dinner. She remained unobtrusive, for the focus of attention was—as it should be—on Tina. For herself she was more than happy to stay on the sidelines, and take care of Ari.

The following day was very similar, with Tina's family

relaxing, making the villa seem very full. Sam came over for lunch, and Ari was in his element, introducing him to any of Tina's family who had not already met him.

'This is Dr Sam.' He beamed. 'He is not a sore tummy doctor. He is an old things doctor. Very old things. Older than Ya-ya.'

This, of course, drew amused laughter—including from Mrs Theakis. She was being—Ann would never have thought otherwise—an exceptionally kindly hostess to her new guests. But what Ann also had to acknowledge was that so was her son. He was as welcoming and as pleasant as any guest could wish. There was no trace of arrogance about him, nothing of the rich man condescending to his employee's relations.

Ann found herself watching him. She told herself she was merely watching *out* for him—making sure she kept a physical distance from him, making sure she said nothing that might draw his unwelcome attention to her. But she knew it was more than that. She knew that seeing him talking, smiling—even laughing—his manner relaxed and easy, was doing things to her insides.

Like tying them into knots. Tight knots. Squeezing hard.

Deliberately she stayed at the edges of the company and the conversation, effacing herself as much as she could. This worked until Tina's mother, directly addressing her, said, 'Tina says she is so relieved you are here, Ann—to take Ari's mind off the fact that she is leaving.'

Ann smiled a little ruefully, first glancing to see that Ari himself was out of earshot, his eyes only for the radio controlled car that Tina's parents had brought for him as a present.

'Tina must not worry too much. Ari will get used to her absence,' she said. 'It may sound upsetting to an adult, but at his age he will adapt very quickly to new circumstances.'

'I do hope you are right,' said Tina's mother doubtfully.

Ann sought to reassure her. 'Well, I lost my mother at four—Ari's age. And I have to say I have almost no memories of her—certainly not of losing her. My "memories" of her are really my sister's. She told me about her. It was much worse for Carla—Ari's mother. She was nearly nine, and felt our mother's death very badly.'

'Oh, how very sad! And for your father, of course.'

'He wasn't there any more. He left when I was born,' replied Ann.

'Good heavens—how dreadful for you two girls, left alone. What happened to you?'

Ann didn't really want to answer Tina's mother's enquiry, but it was made with concern and sympathy, so she answered briefly. 'We were fostered. Luckily Carla and I were able to stay together, which doesn't always happen when children are taken into care.'

Tina's mother smiled sympathetically. 'You must have been very close to your sister?'

'Yes.'

It was all Ann could say. She looked away—and found her gaze colliding, as if with a stone wall, with Nikos'. He was looking at her, his expression strange. She snapped her eyes away immediately, and to her relief Mrs Theakis moved the conversation onwards again.

Tina's wedding day dawned as another beautifully warm and sunny day, with the villa and its beautiful gardens creating a fairytale setting. With the civil ceremony having been conducted on Maxos, for the Greek authorities, Tina and Sam returned to the villa later in the day for an Anglican blessing, held under a vast gazebo erected on the largest terrace and conducted by Sam's uncle, a Church of England canon, attended by all their family and friends, as well as the Theakis family.

Ann sat beside Mrs Theakis, with little Ari, very smartly dressed, on her lap. Less happily, Nikos was on her other side. She sat very stiffly, drawing herself away from him, but his presence was overpowering all the same, and she was horribly conscious of it through the ceremony. But not enough to distract her from the beauty of the ceremony itself. Canon Forbes blessed the bridal couple and at the end, as Ann watched Sam's strong hands gently cradling Tina's face to kiss it, gazing down with love and happiness reflected like a shining mirror from his bride's eyes, she felt her own swell with tears. She had held them at bay throughout the service, but now they spilled over. Silently they coursed down her cheeks. Surreptitiously she dashed them away with her finger. Then, a moment later, a large silk handkerchief was pressed silently into her hand.

'My mother and Eupheme came better prepared,' said a low, deep voice at her ear.

Ann glanced at the older women, and indeed, as Nikos had indicated, both were shedding unashamed tears of emotion, delicately mopped with lawn handkerchiefs. As her gaze moved back to the bridal couple it brushed past Nikos. For a second she wasn't sure she could credit what she thought she had just seen in his face as he stared at Tina and Sam. Some strong emotion she could put no name to. Then, as she was still staring, his gaze suddenly flicked back to her.

The same emotion was still in it.

CHAPTER TEN

THE WEDDING RECEPTION was a lavish affair. Everyone was in evening dress, and Ann, though she wished she had another dress to wear, had no option but to put on Carla's dress. When she did, gazing at herself, her hair dressed in a low chignon at the nape of her neck, she was glad. It was a beautiful dress! And she knew she looked beautiful in it.

If there were dark associations with it, she would ignore them.

Just as she would ignore the man who had told her about them.

As she had been since Tina's family had arrived, Ann was glad to be unobtrusive, looking after Ari. Glad too that Nikos was spending his time being a highly hospitable host, which kept him well away from her. After the lengthy wedding dinner came dancing under the stars. Ari, though getting sleepy, wanted to dance, and Ann smilingly obliged, letting him lead her out importantly, and count with great concentration the '*one,* two, three' of the slow waltz being played as she held out her hands and he lifted his to hers. The steps brought them close to Tina—who was dancing, Ann realised too late, with Nikos, while her new husband bestowed his favours on one of the other female guests.

'Oh, Ari,' cried Tina laughingly. 'Dancing with Auntie Annie and not with me! I'm jealous!'

Immediately Ari let go of Ann. 'Tina is next,' he explained to her, and defected to his nanny. Tina disengaged from Nikos and swept off with Ari. Ann made to slip away, but suddenly her wrist was taken.

'I believe we have changed partners,' he said.

And took her in his arms.

It was done in a moment. She could not stop him without tugging free, making a scene. And she couldn't—not now, at Tina's wedding. But her body had gone rigid instantly, stiffening like steel. It annoyed him, she could tell, for his eyes had darkened, his mouth had tightened. She didn't care, though. Why should she? And anyway, she must not look at him—must not let her eyes anywhere near his face, which was so close, must not meet his gaze, above all must not be conscious in any way whatsoever of the touch of his hand at her waist, his clasp of her hand. She mustn't—just mustn't.

But it was useless. Every cell in her body screamed to her of his closeness, the warmth of his body, the firm pressure of the hand at her waist, guiding her steps, the warm touch of the hand holding hers as they turned—she stiffly, he with the same fluid grace that she had last seen when he'd joined his countrymen dancing in the taverna.

The night he'd seduced her…

Weakness rushed through her, and if her limbs hadn't been as stiff as steel she would have collapsed, falling forward against him, requiring his strength to effortlessly support her.

The music lilted through her brain, her blood, and the rhythm turned them so that imperceptibly, treacherously, she felt it loosen her limbs, dissolving their stiff rigidity—seducing her all on its own.

He felt it—his hand tightened at her waist, ineluctably drawing her against him. She tried to counter by bringing the hand she was holding inwards, as if to ward him off, but it only meant that his clasp enfolded her hand the more, and worse—worse—caught their hands between her breast and his chest. Desperately she found her other hand clutching at his shoulder, at the smooth, rich material of his tuxedo jacket.

Her heart had started to slug. She could not stop it.

Nor could she stop her head tilting, her eyes going to his.

And drowning.

And it was bliss—magical, beautiful, wonderful!—to be held in his arms and wafted around the floor, the soft folds of her chiffon rustling and lifting and floating, the lush, seductive strains of the music cradling her even as his arms cradled her.

She couldn't resist it. Couldn't! Had no strength, no will. None. So she gave herself to it.

How long the dance lasted she could not tell, because she had stepped out of time. And not just out of time—out of reality. The reality of what had happened between her and Nikos—the sordid reality of what he thought of her—the angry, bitter reality of her loathing of him—seemed to have vanished. While the music lasted reality was banished. Only the magic remained—the magic of being in his arms, his embrace, of gazing up at him, lips parted, as his eyes fixed on hers in that wonderful, magical, drowning gaze that absorbed everything that existed.

Then, out of nowhere, the music stopped—and so did the magic. Blinking, she realised she had stopped moving, become aware of the world again, of the other people there and little Ari, tugging at her dress.

Dazed, unfocussed, she looked down. Ari's face was alight with excitement.

'The fireworks are starting!' He tugged her towards the stone balustrade looking out over the sea in the direction of Maxos.

There was a sudden 'whoosh' and a collective gasp—including a squeal from Ari—and the fireworks started. It was a spectacular display, probably visible from Maxos, and Ann appreciated that it was a generous gesture by the Theakis family to the townsfolk, as well as to Tina and Sam. It went on for ages, dazzling the night sky, and Ann was grateful. It gave her time to try and calm down—not that it ever stopped her being punishingly aware of Nikos, so close to her. But since he was holding Ari, who was squealing in excited delight throughout, at least it meant he couldn't try and touch her.

But would he want to, anyway? Since she had refused his diamonds he had not made the slightest attempt to come near her. He was obviously perfectly happy to go off with the likes of Elena Constantis—and who knew how many other women?

So why had he danced with her?

There had been no reason for him to take her in his arms and waltz with her, as if…as if… She felt her heart squeeze suddenly, painfully. As if it were the most romantic thing in the world— the most magical, the most wonderful. The pain clutched her again. As if he had never offered her a diamond necklace for sex and told her she was a hypocrite not to take it…

That was what she must remember! Nothing else! Not those few stupid, foolish minutes in his arms as the lilting music had danced in her veins and the magic had woven its velvet dreams into her head.

With a stupendous crescendo the fireworks ended. Ann turned away from the balcony and saw that Ari was almost asleep on Nikos's chest.

'Bedtime, poppet,' she said, and moved reluctantly to take him from Nikos.

'I'll carry him,' came the reply, and he started to thread his way towards the French windows leading inside. 'He's already asleep.'

Ann followed him inside. She'd half thought to stay out with the party, simply to keep away from Nikos, but Ari had reached out a hand for her.

'Auntie Annie put me to bed,' he said drowsily, but with a plaintive note. So she followed Nikos, her chiffon skirts sussurrating.

It was so quiet in the nursery quarters—and quite deserted. She found herself tensing, realising how alone she was here with Nikos.

It took only a very little time to see Ari into bed. He was already asleep as Nikos laid him carefully down, then stepped away to let Ann gently ease him into his pyjamas, lightly sponging his face and hands, then tucking him in with his teddy. For a moment, forgetting Nikos' presence, she soothed Ari's hair, feeling the soft silkiness beneath her fingers. His lashes were so long, she thought—almost as long as his uncle's…

She bent to drop a silent kiss on Ari's forehead, then straightened. Nikos was standing at the foot of Ari's bed, watching her. For a moment—a strange, breathless moment— she met his eyes. The light was dim, with only Ari's night-light on. She could not read the expression in his face, or in his eyes, knew only that she could not look away.

It was not like any look they had exchanged before. This was—different. She didn't know why, could only feel the difference. Feel the vibration that went through her—not just through her body, but somewhere deeper.

Then Ari stirred in his sleep and the moment was gone. Leaving only a whisper behind of an emotion she could not name. Different from any she had ever known. It was strange—disturbing. And something more. Something had seemed to come like a lift to her heart, like music she had never heard before, impressing deep upon her…haunting her like a ghost—a ghost of something that had never been…. could never be.

Jerkily, she moved to shake out and fold Ari's clothes, smoothing their creases and draping them over a chair. It was displacement activity, she knew. To give her time to recover her composure after that strange, disturbing moment—and more practically, to give Nikos time to leave.

But when she could no longer keep smoothing Ari's clothes she had to turn round—to see, with a quiver going through her, that Nikos had not moved. He was still standing there, watching her.

She made herself speak. 'You can go back to the party. I'm staying with Ari. I moved my things into Tina's room so as to be next door to him.' Her words sounded dislocated, disjointed. Awkward.

A second later she wished them desperately unsaid. Oh, God, had he thought she was telling him deliberately where she was going to sleep, hoping he'd come to her? Or, worse, would he now think he could?

But he didn't reply to what she had said. Instead, his eyes still resting on her, he spoke. His voice was low, grating— almost reluctant, as if he spoke against his will.

'You were right to wear that dress. You look—breathtaking.' There was a pause—minute, but telling. 'Nothing like your sister looked in it. Nothing at all…' His voice seemed to trail away.

She couldn't speak, did not know what to say. The silence stretched between them, the tension thick. For a moment longer he just went on standing there, looking at her, as she stood immobile, motionless. Then, with the slightest alteration of expression, his gaze loosed hers at last and he left the room.

For quite some time Ann could only stand there, still immobile. There seemed to be a hollow somewhere inside her, but she wasn't sure where.

Or why.

Nikos stood on the terrace outside his bedroom, his hands curved over the stone balustrade, looking out to sea. The scent of jasmine and honeysuckle caught at his senses. And not just at his senses—his memory. How short a time ago he had stood here with Ann, waiting to take her into his arms, his bed, seducing her in the sweet Aegean night—

He had not wanted the music to end. He had not wanted to let her go. She had seemed so—different. Not the woman he knew her to be. And just now, when he'd watched her put Ari to bed, how tenderly she'd kissed him, how naturally her affection for him had seemed to show. It had made strange, disquieting thoughts form in his head. Questions he wanted her to answer—but why he wanted her to answer them he would not ask himself.

He went on gazing out over the sea, disturbed, unsettled. Restless.

The next day seemed very flat, and when Tina's family had left after lunch, profusely thanking Mrs Theakis and Nikos for their wonderful hospitality, it seemed even flatter. Ari felt it most, Ann knew.

The reality of Tina actually leaving was hitting him, and though Ann reassured him that she was only on her honeymoon, and would be back soon from a Nile cruise, he was fretful and disconsolate—tired, too, after his exciting day and very late night. She was patient and forbearing with him, but it was hard going.

At least she didn't have to face Nikos, however. Once lunch was over and Tina's family had left for the rest of their holiday, at a popular resort on another Greek island, he kept to his office.

The next day was easier, with Ann getting Ari to draw pictures of Tina and Sam beside huge pyramids. But Ann was worried about him. Who would look after him when she herself had gone—as go, soon, she surely must? It would not be kind to stay so long that Ari got too used to her...

But at lunchtime Sophia Theakis dropped a bombshell.

'Now, Ari, my darling,' she said, smiling mysteriously, 'there is a wonderful surprise in store for you. A holiday, just for you!'

Ari's eyes were huge with excitement. 'Where? Where?' he cried.

Ann could only stare, wonderingly. She realised that Nikos had paused at the head of the table, and was staring equally bemused at his mother. He started to speak, clearly wanting to know more, but his mother silenced him by addressing her grandson.

'Somewhere little boys will *love* to go! You are going—' her eyes twinkled even more '—with Uncle Nikos and Auntie Annie to the best theme park in Paris!'

Immediately Ari cried out in blissful glee—but his uncle cut right across him. The Greek that followed was intense on his part and unruffled on his mother's—she was adamant. As for Ann, she could only sit there in disbelieving dismay. Her mind raced frantically. Of course Ari's grandmother could have no idea—none at all!—just *why* it was so impossible, so completely, utterly impossible, for her and Nikos to go off together with Ari.

The moment lunch was over, Ann handed Ari to Maria and hurried to Nikos' office. She didn't want to—the last thing she wanted to do was speak to him deliberately, let alone in the place where he had so cruelly offered her diamonds for sex—but there was no alternative.

At his desk, Nikos knew it was going to be Ann at the door—and he knew why. 'Come in.' His command was terse, and as she marched inside her expression was grim.

'I am *not* going to Paris with you!' she said immediately.

Just as immediately, Nikos found his own expression hardening. Gone in a flash was that unsettling sense of there having been something different about Ann. He was back on familiar territory again. All too familiar. Ann Turner defying him. Refusing him. Refusing to hand over her baby nephew.

Refusing to come out to Sospiris at his mother's invitation. Refusing to admit she wanted him. Refusing to accept his diamonds—refusing, now, to go to Paris with him...

Always damn well refusing him!

He was fed up to the back teeth with it all. He leant back in his leather chair, hands resting palm-down on the surface of the desk.

'I have no intention,' he spelt out, eyeballing her, 'of having my mother upset. Nor Ari. So you'll come with us to Paris, and that is all there is to it.'

Her eyes flashed furiously. 'You cannot *possibly* want to do what your mother's planned? You objected fast enough when she announced it!'

He had. It was true. An instinctive objection, and one that he had not been able to express in any way other than by claiming pressure of work. But his mother had calmly informed him that she'd checked with his PA and been told that there was no pressing business to prevent him taking time out for the coming week.

'I repeat,' he said brusquely, 'I will not have my mother upset. Nor Ari. We have no alternative but to go through with this farce. God knows—' his voice was edged suddenly '—it's been a farce right from the start!' He took a short breath, silencing her evident desire to riposte by raising a hand peremptorily. 'However,' he continued, 'from Paris you will go back to London. You've already spent more time with Ari than is good for him. Now, that is all there is to be said on the subject. And since,' he finished with heavy mordancy, 'I am to be away from my desk from tomorrow, I have a great deal of work to get through today!'

It was a dismissal, and he looked at her pointedly. For a moment she just stood there, visibly fulminating.

'Ann,' he said, and there was something in his voice that crawled over her skin, 'if you are waiting for me to make you a cash offer for your compliance, you will, I warn you, be disappointed. You've already been paid for your time with my family—consider Paris as part of that holiday.'

His eyes rested on her, and for a moment two spots of colour burned in her cheeks as her lips pressed together tightly. Then, without a further word, she turned on her heel and left.

CHAPTER ELEVEN

'COME *ON*, AUNTIE Annie! Come *on!*' Ari's piping voice was breathless with excitement. Ann finished replaiting her hair, and smiled down at him.

'Nearly ready. Why not go and check if your uncle is?'

Ari zoomed off to the connecting suite in the hotel, repeating his urging. Ann took a big breath to steady herself. She was here, in Paris, about to set off for the theme park—and she was with Nikos. She didn't want to be, but she was. And she just had to cope.

Somehow.

Ari, however, was of course ecstatic with excitement as they made their way into the heartland of any child's dreams. Open-mouthed, he stared around, exclaiming at every scene.

In the central concourse, Nikos hunkered down beside him with the park map opened out. 'OK, Ari, what ride do you want to do first?'

There followed two hours of breathless bliss for Ari, though for Ann, on those rides where Ari was snuggled between them, she felt that Nikos was far too physically close to her—especially when his arm reached around the back of the car, dangerously near her shoulders. But for Ari's sake she bore it stoically and tried not to tense too obviously.

And yet Nikos, she noticed, seemed to take her presence in his stride. She knew she was doing it for Ari, but Ann found, against her will, that as the afternoon wore on her tension was wearing off. She even caught herself exchanging amused smiles with Nikos when Ari made some childish expression of delight.

As the afternoon waned, Ari started to flag. Nikos hefted him up on his shoulders, and they made their way to the exit, buying a helium-filled balloon on route. Back at the hotel, Nikos had booked Ari a 'fun tea,' and afterwards, tired out from all the excitement, he went willingly to bed.

'Asleep?' The deep voice sounded from the communicating doorway.

Ann stood up from where she had been sitting on Ari's bed. She nodded.

'Exhausted by an excess of fun,' said Nikos. He strolled in and looked down at the sleeping boy. Something shifted in his eyes suddenly.

'I see Andreas in him—' He stopped. As if he had said what he shouldn't. His tone changed, deliberately lightening. 'He's had a good day—no doubt about that.'

'Yes,' said Ann. Her voice was stilted. It was the first time she had been in Nikos's company today without Ari's presence as an essential diversion.

'I've ordered dinner to be served in my suite in about an hour. That way we don't have to worry about organising a babysitting service—just keep the communicating door open.'

'Oh,' said Ann. She hadn't really known what to expect. Obviously she didn't actually want to have dinner with Nikos, but at least there would be waiting staff present.

But when, having spent the hour having a bath, she nerved herself to go through, it was to find that no servers were present. The table was beautifully laid, the first course set out already, and the second course was being kept hot on a side table. Almost she retreated, then steeled herself. She could get through this if she tried.

Nikos was pouring from a bottle of wine. He didn't ask whether Ann wanted any, just set a full glass at her place opposite him. He must have showered, Ann realised, for his hair was damply feathering, and he was freshly shaved too. He'd changed into an open necked shirt and dark blue trousers. He looked—she gulped silently—devastating.

But then he always did! It didn't matter what or where or when! He always, *always* made her stomach hollow.

Always had. Always would.

She picked up her knife and fork and started to eat her first course.

'No toast?'

She paused, looking up. 'What?'

Nikos picked up his wine glass. 'To Ari's holiday.'

It was impossible to disagree. Reluctantly she picked up her wine glass, and took a small sip in acknowledgement.

'One thing I'll say for you freely, Ann—you make an effort for him.'

'It would be hard not to,' she answered quietly. It was bizarre to hear a compliment, however mild, come out of Nikos.

'Yes,' he agreed. He paused. 'I hope the menu is to your liking?'

'Oh, yes, it's fine. Thank you. It's delicious.'

'Better than in the park,' he commented wryly.

'Well, I suppose they are catering for children, so fast food is the order of the day. The ice-creams were good, though.'

'Ari certainly thought so. Though he got most of it on his face!'

She smiled. 'I think a lot reached his tummy too.'

'It didn't stop him putting away a good tea, all the same.'

'No—having fun must make you extra hungry.'

'And sleepy. He was out like a light.'

'Recharging his batteries. Ready for tomorrow.'

It was so strange—exchanging pleasantries like this, even stilted ones. But what was the alternative? Ripping apart the frail veneer that kept them civil like this? Dragging everything vicious and ugly that lay between them back out into the open? No, better—easier—to do what she was doing now. What she had done all day since they'd left Sospiris. Behave as though the enmity between them did not exist.

'What's the schedule for tomorrow?' she ventured. 'By the way, I should point out to you that Ari has spotted there's a swimming pool in the hotel!'

A smile tugged at Nikos's mouth. Ann tried not to think how it made her stomach tug too.

'Are you volunteering me?' he asked, eyebrows raising with quizzical humour.

'No, I don't mind taking him in the least. I want to make the most of him while I—' She broke off. She had been refusing to let herself think that these were the last few days she would have with Ari, not knowing when she might see him again—or even if. No! She mustn't think like that. Ari's grandmother had promised, as Ann had taken leave of her that morning, that she would not lose touch. But would Nikos let that happen? Anxiety gnawed at her.

She looked down, continuing with her eating. Nikos made no reply, just watched her mechanically lifting her fork to her mouth and back.

She was back to being different again. It was because of Ari, he knew. That was obvious. When the boy was there she slipped into the 'different' Ann that she had started to be during Tina's wedding. A frown creased his brow as memory teased at him. She'd made some remark to Tina's mother—something that had struck him at the time. He reached for his wine and took a draught.

'You said you lost your mother when you were young?'

The words came out balder than he'd intended. Her head snapped up. She looked taken aback, and momentarily blank.

'You said it to Tina's mother,' he prompted.

Ann frowned. 'What of it?' Why on earth had he suddenly said that? Out of nowhere.

'You said you were taken into care?'

Ann stiffened. 'Yes. Why do you ask?'

He was looking at her strangely. 'Because I realise how little I know about you, Ann.'

'Why should you want to?' she countered. Nikos Theakis knew all he considered he needed to know about her. Why should he suddenly want to know more? What for? He'd never evinced the slightest interest before—why now?

'Because—' Nikos began, then stopped. Why *did* he want to know? What was it to him what Ann Turner's background was? What her childhood had been? It was irrelevant—she was the person she was. That was all. Desirable, hypocritical, venal. He had proof of all those three qualities. They were enough for any woman!

But was it enough for him to know? Was there more about her?

'You said something about foster parents?' The prompting came again.

'Yes.' It was a bald reply, and all he got.

'Were they good to you?' Why had he said that? Why did he care?

She gave a little shrug. 'Some were better than others.'

He frowned. 'You had more than one set?'

'We were moved at least three times. The last—' She broke off.

'Yes?'

Unconsciously Ann reached for her wine and took a mouthful. She needed it.

'The last placement was very good for me. I thrived. I was

happiest there. The foster mother was kind, and I liked her. The foster father—' She broke off again. Took another mouthful of wine.

'The foster father…?' Again Nikos was prompting her.

Something flashed in her eyes. Hard. Like a knife-blade. He wanted to know? OK, he could know. 'The foster father was fine—with me.' She took a constricted breath that razored in her throat. She breathed out harshly. 'That was because I was too young for him. He liked young teenage girls—like Carla.'

Nikos's expression had stilled. 'Are you saying—?' he said slowly.

'Yes.' It was all she said. All she had to say.

'But surely there were social workers for you both, if you were in state care? Why didn't your sister—?'

Ann's gaze was unblinking. 'Carla didn't tell them. She knew I was happy in that placement. So for my sake she…put up with it. She didn't want us moved again, unsettled. And the risk of separation was always there. It's hard for fostered siblings to be kept together—there's such a shortage of foster carers. She thought that at least we were together, and that— well, she could stick it out. So she did. For two years. Until she was old enough to leave at sixteen.' A final breath exhaled from her. 'Then she got out of there like a bat out of hell. But not before telling our foster father that she would be keeping a lookout for me like a hawk, and if he made the slightest move on me now that I was older she'd see him in jail. So he never touched me—and I never knew about what had happened to Carla until I was old enough to leave care. I found out when Carla called the social workers in, and the police, and got the man prosecuted. So he couldn't prey on any other girls they took in.'

Nikos paused. 'His wife colluded?'

Ann shook her head. 'She didn't know. She really, really didn't know. When the case came to court, and Carla and I had to give our testimony, she looked as if her very soul had been destroyed. It was heartbreaking for her. She felt guilty because she'd failed to care for the children in her charge, because she'd been so blind to her husband's nature.'

Nikos was silent. Silenced. Ann had resumed eating. Focussing only on her food, her face blank. Slowly, he spoke.

'I didn't know.' The words seemed inadequate even as he said them.

Ann glanced at him. 'Why should you? If you want to apply popular psychology you could say that because a man used Carla she decided that in future she'd use them. Which she did. Does it excuse her? I don't know.'

'Perhaps,' said Nikos slowly, as if his thoughts were rearranging themselves in his head, 'it explains her.'

'Maybe it does. But then maybe she just wanted the good things in life. We weren't materially deprived in care, but we didn't have anything of our own. Carla was always hungry for material goods. Maybe she wanted to taste luxury the easy way.'

His expression had changed. He was looking at her. Different thoughts were in his head now. Memory was suddenly vivid in his mind. Four years ago he'd stood in Ann Turner's dingy flat and seen only a place utterly unfit in which to bring up his brother's son. His only urge had been to get Ari out of there. Now, in his mind's eye, he saw it differently. As the place Ann had *had* to live in. The rundown area, the shabby furniture, the primitive kitchen, worn carpets, peeling wallpaper—all the signs of poverty and squalor.

No wonder she had wanted out...

His eyes rested on her as she went on eating.

If I'd been as poor as she was, would I, too, have been tempted to do what she did...sell Ari for a million?

The thought sat in his head with a weight he did not want to feel. But felt all the same.

What did he know of poverty? He'd been born to immense wealth, immense privilege. What must it be like to have to live in a place like that? To have your world confined to such conditions? Dreary, cramped, dingy, squalid.

And then someone offered you a million pounds...

So you could taste luxury the easy way...

Ann had finished eating, setting aside her knife and fork. She lifted her head.

'Would you like me to serve the next course?'

Her voice was quite steady, as if they had not just been talking about what had happened to her sister as a vulnerable young teenager.

Nikos nodded. 'Yes, thank you.'

She busied herself clearing away their plates and moving to the sideboard. Nikos joined her, lifting the lids of the chafing dishes. His thoughts were troubled, confused. Unsettling. Making him think things he found uncomfortable.

Briskly, Ann took the filled plates back to the table. Nikos poured out more wine. They settled down to eat the next course. After a few moments Ann said, 'There are several shows on in the park that I'm sure Ari would love. If you can't face them I can take him, if you like.'

'No, the pleasure is in seeing his pleasure,' returned Nikos.

He spoke in a deliberately easy manner. It was clear that Ann wanted to change the subject, and he could understand why. But even as they resumed their deliberately light conversation about Ari his thoughts were running as a background process in his mind. Like an underground river— eroding what he had taken for the solid rock of his certainties about her. Her sister.

He thought of what he'd known of Carla Turner. Yet she had protected her young sister's happiness by sacrificing herself to the lusts of a pervert exploiting the very children he had been appointed to care for. Had that loss of innocence she'd suffered made her the woman she'd become? Irremediably scarred by what a man had done to her?

And Ann? What of her? Taking the money he'd offered her as her only chance to escape the poverty she'd been trapped in?

Again he felt the certainties he had held for so long shift, become unstable. Reshape themselves.

But what shape would they finally take? He did not know. Could not tell. Could only let them run in the background of his mind while he dined with a woman he both desired and despised.

The next day was spent entirely at Ari's pleasure: a second visit to the theme park, a swim in the hotel pool, and a dare-devil circus dinner show in the evening. Then came a day at a second theme park, rounded off with a candlelit parade and supper at the main park. Back in their suite, Ari was asleep in minutes.

Ann kissed him tenderly, an ache filling her heart. This was their last day here—which meant tomorrow she must return to London. Leave Ari.

Leave Nikos—

The ache in her heart seemed to intensify…

'Come and have some coffee.' Nikos's deep voice came from the doorway. She straightened, composing herself. Her expression did not falter even as her eyes went straight to Nikos'. As if a magnet drew them thither.

But then he drew *all* women's eyes.

She went through to the reception room. After all, this would be the last time she would spend with him. The sense of loss increased even as she berated herself for letting it in.

'So,' said Nikos, relaxing back, taking his coffee cup, 'do you think Ari is theme parked out?'

She made her voice sound normal—the way she had done all the time here. 'For now, yes. But as soon as you get him home he'll be asking you when you're going to take him again!'

He laughed, and Ann had to drop her eyes. The aching feeling inside her was getting stronger. She must crush it. Because there was no place for it. This time tomorrow she would be back in London, with her own life—her real life—taking her over again. That was what she must remember.

Remember what Nikos Theakis thought of her…

'Well, next year, perhaps,' he allowed. 'But I admit I'm looking forward to being in central Paris tomorrow. Tell me, do you know the city?'

She shook her head. 'I've never been there.'

'Never been?' He sounded surprised, as if it were odd she'd never been. 'Well, then, it will be my pleasure to show the city to you both—you and Ari.'

She swallowed. 'It might be better if I got a midday flight back to London,' she said. 'I don't want to arrive too late.'

He was looking at her. His eyes were veiled suddenly. 'Ari's holiday is not yet over,' he said. 'There is no question of you abandoning him yet.'

'I didn't mean I wanted to leave him,' she said defensively.

For a moment his eyes rested on her with that same veiled expression. Then, lifting his coffee cup, he said, 'Good, then that is settled. Tomorrow we remove to central Paris and do our sightseeing.'

Ann felt her mood lift—she knew she shouldn't let it, but it was too late.

A reprieve—

As she thought the word, she wished it unthought. But she knew it was true, for all that.

CHAPTER TWELVE

IF SHE'D WONDERED whether a city with so sophisticated a reputation as Paris might not have much to appeal to a young child, Ann swiftly discovered her mistake. The next day, after they'd taken a taxi into the centre of the city and checked into a hotel so world-famous it made her eyes stretch, Ari could not wait to get out and about.

The Metro was an immediate hit, and so was the Eiffel Tower—especially lunching halfway up. Then came a ride on a *bâteau mouche* on the River Seine, followed by a stroll through the Tuileries gardens, ending up at a café on the Rue de Rivoli, where Ari wolfed down an ice-cream, and Ann contented herself with a *café au lait,* nobly resisting the mouthwatering array of patisserie—which Nikos, to her chagrin, did not.

'You should succumb to temptation, Ann,' he murmured, his eyes glinting.

She pressed her lips together. Why couldn't Nikos be the way he'd been on Sospiris—raking at her, castigating her sister, insulting her with diamonds? Why did he have to be like this now, with that lazy glint in his eye and his casual companionableness, and their mutual conspiracy towards Ari that they were the best of friends? Making remarks that sounded innocuous but which carried a subtext a mile high?

Was he doing it on purpose? she wondered bleakly. Baiting her? Taunting her? Yet the humour in his glint belied so malign a purpose. Hinting at a purpose that made her insides give a little skip.

But what was the point? What was the point of reacting to the male gorgeousness that was Nikos Theakis? She was here with him for Ari's sake, that was all. She forced her heart to harden. Nothing could take away the poison that lay between them, however superficially nice Nikos was being.

Yet that evening, with Ari fast asleep in the exquisitely appointed bedroom Ann shared with him in the suite Nikos had taken for them all, the soft knock on her door took her by surprise.

'We can dine downstairs,' Nikos informed her. 'I've booked one of the hotel's babysitters to be up here until we return. And since, Ann, this is a grand hotel, we shall dine in grand style.' His eyes held hers a moment—a brief, dangerous moment. 'Wear the turquoise evening gown again—you won't be overdressed, I promise you.'

She should, she knew, have made some excuse. Pleaded a headache, or tiredness—anything to avoid dining with Nikos Theakis *en grande tenue* at this world famous hotel in the heart of Paris. And yet she didn't.

He certainly drew all eyes as they made their way into the three-Michelin-starred restaurant at the hotel. But then Nikos Theakis in a tuxedo was a sight to rivet female eyes for miles around.

For herself, she had definitely had to *avert* her gaze, as her eyes had gone to him in the suite, taking in in an instant just how much the superbly tailored jacket enhanced his superbly structured torso, how the gleaming white of his shirt emphasised the sleek muscled chest, and the immaculate dark trousers sheathed his long legs. Keeping her composure in the face of such incentive to lose it had helped minimise the impact of his own sweeping glance over her, wearing once more, as she had done for Tina's wedding reception, the beautiful layered chiffon gown that fell in Grecian folds to her ankles, skimming her breasts and baring one shoulder. She'd dressed her hair loose tonight, and it cascaded down her back, loosely pulled around her bared shoulder. Her make-up, too, she'd applied with particular care—this was, after all, Paris, which must put any woman on her mettle. Especially when she was dining with so superb a specimen of manhood as she was tonight.

The food, she discovered, entirely justified the prestige which the restaurant was held, and when it came to the exquisitely prepared creamy *bavarois,* adorned with a net of spun sugar and laced with vividly hued coulis, she did not hesitate. She dipped her spoon into the heavenly concoction—only to find Nikos's amused, long-lashed gaze on her.

'Enjoy,' he murmured, and his eyes gave their familiar glint.

She felt her breath catch in her throat, two flares of colour flag in her cheeks, then she dipped her head to taste the mouthful of dessert. It was as gorgeous to eat as to look at, and it did not last long. She surfaced to see Nikos still watching with amusement, lounging back in his seat, a glass of Sauternes between his fingers.

But even as she met his gaze it changed. Amusement flickered to something else, and now the catch in Ann's throat was enough to still her breath. Then, abruptly, the gaze was gone. He took a mouthful of his wine, his gaze turned inward. Then that expression, too, changed.

'So—' he tilted his chair further back, easing his shoulders more, relaxation in every line of his lithe, powerful body '—what shall we do tomorrow, Ann?'

'Anywhere by Metro will keep Ari happy.' She smiled, grateful for the safety of talking about Ari instead of having Nikos looking at her with his long-lashed, gold-glinting eyes.

'I just hope he doesn't realise one can take the Metro all the way back out to the theme parks!' said Nikos feelingly.

She laughed. 'Ari heaven! But then this whole holiday has been wonderful for him! Any child would have adored it.'

For a moment there was a shadow in her eyes. It was only fleeting, but Nikos noticed it, all the same.

'What is it?' he asked.

She gave a half smile, a little rueful. 'He doesn't know how fortunate he is, compared with so many other children.'

Nikos's face was sombre a moment. 'True, he has every material blessing. But no parents.'

Ann bit her lip. 'Yes, but there are many children with neither families nor material security. Still,' she went on, 'who would begrudge him for a second the happiness he has? And he isn't spoilt—not in the slightest.'

'No,' agreed Nikos. 'He isn't. We have done our best, myself, my mother and Tina, to ensure he is not a spoilt brat.'

'Never!' exclaimed Ann feelingly. 'He's an angelic child.'

There was a tug at Nikos' mouth. 'Now, there speaks a doting aunt!' Then, as it had before, his expression changed. 'And you are, aren't you, Ann? It's not a show for my benefit, is it? You really do love him.'

'Is that so surprising?' she asked steadily.

His eyes rested on her, with that same expression in them that she could not read. 'Perhaps not,' he answered.

Was there reluctance in his voice? Of course there must be, thought Ann. It would gall him to think she really cared for the nephew she had sold, as he so scathingly reminded her whenever it suited him, for hard cash.

And suddenly, out of nowhere, Ann found herself wanting to dispel that view of her as heartless and mercenary.

'I think you have come to love Ari,' he said slowly. 'Being with him as you have been on Sospiris and here, now, day after day. I think you have come to love him now that he is no longer a baby—a burden on your life imposed on you by your sister's death, a responsibility you could not evade.'

His eyes were resting on her, still with that unreadable expression in them, and Ann could only let him speak—even though she wanted to shout out that he was wrong, *wrong!* That she had never, ever regarded Ari as a burden, that he had been the most precious thing in her life, and that giving him up had nearly broken her…

But Nikos was still speaking, his tone sombre, and as she listened her eyes widened in amazement.

'When I came to you that night, Ann, four years ago, fresh off the plane, I'd spent the entire journey in a state of agonising grief for my brother's death. There was only one other emotion in me.' He looked at her, his eyes heavy. 'Fear,' he said.

She stared, not understanding.

'Yes, fear. And anger—not just at your sister, for what she'd done to my brother, but at myself. Harsh, unforgiving anger. Because…' He took a ragged breath. 'It was I who had ensured that Ari was illegitimate. I was so sure that Carla had lied through her teeth to Andreas that she was pregnant by him, and not any of the dozens of men she got through, I persuaded him to wait until the child was born and only then have DNA tests done—convinced as I was that they would be negative, and he would not need to marry a woman like her and ruin his life. So when I arrived that night, Ann, my anger at myself for having myself ensured my dead brother's son was a bastard warred only with my fear—my fear of you.'

'Me?' Ann's voice was disbelieving.

Long lashes swept down over his eyes, and his mouth twisted.

'Yes, Ann—you. A drab slip of a girl, living in a dingy slum, holding a baby in her arms that I desperately, desperately wanted—needed!—and which you could have denied me.' He took another heavy breath. 'Surely, Ann, you knew how powerful your position was? The moment I showed my hand and told you I wanted to take Ari you must have known?'

'Known what?' she said blankly.

'That you were holding me to ransom! *Theos mou*, Ann—you had legal possession of my brother's son. When your sister was killed you became Ari's legal guardian—and as such, the moment you knew I wanted him, you had unlimited power over me. Had Andreas and Carla been married, I could have wrested Ari from you with ease—what court in the world would have awarded custody to a penniless girl in comparison with what I could offer my nephew? But as Ari's guardian, as you were, you held every card.'

Incredulity flared in her face. He saw it, and gave a brief, hollow laugh.

'I came to you that day with only one weapon in my hand. My money.' His mouth twisted again as he spoke. 'Fear that you would turn me down, laugh in my face, made me harsh to you, Ann. Whatever your sister had done, you were hardly responsible—I knew and accepted that! Yet my anger at her, my fear of you—of the power you held to deny me what I needed most, my brother's son—made me angry with you, too. But...' His eyes closed momentarily as he faced truths he had not wanted to face—truths that told him baldly, bleakly, just why he had so wanted to hate and despise Ann Turner for selling her baby nephew to him. 'I had a lucky escape that day—and do not think I did not know it. I found a woman young enough, poor enough, to bribe with a pittance.'

Ann swallowed. A million pounds? A pittance? But Nikos was talking again. His voice was darkly bitter—at himself.

'Do you not realise how I cheated you that day, Ann? You could have held out for far, far more. I would have given the world for Ari. You could have sent me off, left me to sweat with no room to manoeuvre, once you realised how desperately I wanted Ari. You could have raised the bidding—not just to sell him to me, but for a share in the Theakis wealth. You could have gone to the press, Ann—kicked up a storm, a hideous scandal over our heads, raking up everything your sister had been. You could have hired a team of crack lawyers to get your fingers into the Theakis fortune on behalf of the child for whom you were legal guardian, illegitimate though he was. Just thinking of what you held the power to do that day made me so harsh to you. Even as you took that cheque for a paltry million pounds from my hand I hated you for the power you had over me.'

He stilled, the strong emotion in his face fading—but not completely.

'And I hated you for selling Ari to me—even though it was what I wanted—so swiftly and so cheaply. I've condemned you ever since for it.'

She swallowed. There seemed to be a stone lodged in her throat, making it hard—impossible—to breathe.

'I…I noticed,' she said.

His eyes were on her, heavy, and it was a weight she could scarcely bear.

'But what right have I, Ann—I who have only ever known wealth and ease and luxury, all my life, through no effort of my own, merely inheriting it—what right have I to condemn someone born to poverty for taking easy money when it came their way? Would I, Ann, in your position, have been any more virtuous? Would I have turned down the money dangled so temptingly in front of me so that I could live the rest of my life in poverty? Raising my sister's orphaned child, giving up my life to my nephew just so that his rich uncle would not condemn me? Would I have been any better than you?' He paused. 'I would not like to be put to that test, Ann—as you were.'

Her mouth was working. She had to speak—had to! Had to tell him that—

But Nikos was speaking again. His voice was urgent, suddenly—persuasive. Compelling.

'I want to put it behind us Ann. Nothing—nothing that I've seen of you, known of you, since you came to Sospiris—gives me any further cause to think ill of you. Indeed—' his voice twisted '—you have even proved to me you do not have your sister's morals when it comes to sex, haven't you?'

She felt colour flare out along her cheeks, felt Nikos' gold-glinting eyes rest mordantly on her.

'Was that the moment I was forced to rethink my opinion of you, Ann?' he mused. 'The moment you rejected the diamond necklace I wanted to give you, which I thought you would seize with both your greedy little hands? I didn't want you to reject it—I wanted you to take it.'

'Yes,' she answered tightly, the colour still flaring in her cheeks. 'I'm aware of that.'

His lips twitched. 'Not because I wanted to confirm my low opinion of you, Ann. Because…' The long lashes swept down again, making her breath catch though she shouldn't let it— she shouldn't, she mustn't. 'Because I wanted you back in my bed—any way I could get you there.'

His hand reached across the table. A single finger stroked along the back of her hand. She felt the lightness of his touch as if it were searing heat.

'I still want you, Ann.' His voice was low, intense.

The breath stilled in her lungs. She could not breathe, nor speak, though she should do both…

He was holding her with his gaze, as if her entire weight were suspended. Words came from him, seductive, sensuous.

'You are so beautiful. So incredibly beautiful—'

His eyes swept over her, making her weak—so weak.

But she could not be weak—*must* not. However much her head was swirling with the same overwhelming emotion as when he had danced with her, taken her into his arms in those magical, dreamlike moments.

'It's…it's not a good idea,' she said. Her voice seemed strained, tortured.

But Nikos wasn't listening. His mouth was lowering to hers.

She made one last, frail attempt.

'Ari…' she breathed.

But all at once they had left the restaurant, were standing in the little entrance hallway outside the suite. She was fighting for sanity, but it would not come. It had fled, far away, and she could not get it back. Dimly she heard voices speaking French—one Nikos, the other the hotel babysitter—and then the woman was slipping past her, letting herself out, and Ann could not say a word, not a word, until Nikos came out of the lounge. And then she still could not say a word, could only let him take her hand and lead her across the lounge and into his bedroom.

And there she could speak only one word—only one.

'Nikos,' she breathed.

She was his. His again. But not as she had been before. Because now his heart was not hardened towards her. Now she was not the woman he must take control of to prevent her exploiting him and his mother any further. She was not the woman he'd cynically, deliberately seduced, succumbing to a desire that he'd needed a reason to slake, allowing him to take her, enjoy her—and still despise her.

Now she was his only because he wanted her—wanted to move his hand over her bare shoulder, feeling the softness of her pale skin, easing aside the chiffon material to free her other shoulder so he could glide his lips along it, even as his fingers went to the zip at the back of the dress. He slid it down in one single long movement, so that the dress fell from her in a shimmer of gossamer, and he turned her, boneless in his hands, to face him.

His breath caught. She was so beautiful! Her rounded breasts, bared to him again, were already swelling to his gaze, and the slender pliancy of her waist awaited his caress. Around her hips there was only a wisp of lace, enticing more than it revealed.

She opened to him willingly, ardently, and his mouth played with hers, each touch, each intimate caress, arousing him yet more and more.

And then her fingers were at his throat, teasing apart the tight knot of his dress tie, slipping the buttons of his shirt, first one and then another, until even as he was kissing her she was baring his body for her own delight, easing his shirt from the confines of his belted hips. He revelled in the feel of her delicate fingertips exploring his torso, revelled yet more in the flatness of her palms smoothing over him, and then, pulling away from her, he shrugged off his jacket, the remains of his shirt.

She stood watching him, even as she had watched him strip down on the beach on Sospiris, when he had first realised his own desire for her. His hands went to his waist, unbuckling his belt, slipping the metal hook, the zip…

He watched her watching him…

With a little cry she turned away, as if she had been caught out, guilty, and he gave a laugh, catching her in his arms even as she turned.

'No shyness! This is for us both, my most beautiful Ann…'

He swept her up, taking her across to the bed, pulling back the coverings and lowering her down on to the sheets where she lay, hair spilling like a silvered flag, her pale body exquisitely beautiful to him. Then he stripped off the rest of his clothes and came down beside her.

He feasted on her. Every morsel of her body was his delight, his pleasure, his to enjoy. As was his body for her. Caressing and arousing, he felt the blood pulse strongly in his veins, and desire—strong and untrammelled—coursed powerfully through him. She was everything he wanted—*everything!*

The bounty of her breasts, the glory of her hair, the sweetness of her mouth, the silk of her skin, and—most glorious of all—the richness of her dewing body, opening to his, drawing him in. She clung to him, hands meshed with his so tightly their palms were sealed, her spine arching, lips parted, eyes glazed as she gazed up into his eyes that were devouring hers. And all the time he thrust within her, taking her with him, onwards, onwards to that place that awaited them both.

It took them in, turning the world to searing glory in a heat so fierce he cried out—a low, guttural cry that found an echo, higher, finer, which melded into the fire in which they writhed together.

And then the coming down—the slow, heavy exhaustion of the body that took him back from the furnace and made him fold her sated body to his, panting, breathless, still quivering, clinging to him as if he were the only still point after the passion that had consumed them both.

She lay in the circle of his arms, exhausted, weak, and gradually he could feel his hectic pulse slow. His own breathing started to ease, and his eyelids felt heavy, so very heavy, so that all he could do was pull the covers over them, hold her stilling body more tightly to him yet, and give himself up into the oblivion that reached for him. His last awareness was of how good, how very, very good it felt to have her body so close, so closely entwined with his.

The place it should be.

The place it would be.

CHAPTER THIRTEEN

ARI WAS CHATTERING, telling them all about what he had seen from the rooftop of Notre Dame, and Ann and Nikos were smiling indulgently at him. But beneath the table in the restaurant where they were having lunch, they were holding hands.

Such a simple gesture, thought Ann, and yet it felt so magical.

But then the whole world had turned to magic.

She'd been mad, she knew, to succumb as she had last night. But how could she have resisted? It was impossible to resist Nikos Theakis. Impossible! Even while he had made no secret of his contempt for her it had been all but impossible to resist him—but now... Her insides squeezed flutteringly. Now that he was being so...so *nice* to her, the very thought of trying to resist him was...impossible.

Yet even as she'd given herself to him—unresisting, quickening with a desire that had swept her into his arms, his bed—she'd known not just that she was mad, but that she was lighting a fire that would be far, far harder to douse this time. Before, she had found the strength to resist him in his vileness to her.

But now, how many days—how many nights—did they have left? Nikos had said nothing of how long he wanted to stay in Paris, but Tina would be back from honeymoon soon, and surely then he'd be returning to Greece with Ari?

Perhaps only a few days—only one or two—but I will take

them—take them and not think about anything else—anything else at all!

It was, she knew, the only policy that made sense in the middle of this madness she was permitting. But what else could she do? It was too late now for sanity to prevail. Last night had proved that—overwhelmingly, consumingly—with memories so vivid, so wonderful, she dared not let them into her head now, lest they show blatantly in her eyes, her expression. And then Nikos would know, and then desire would leap between them, as it had done again and again through out the long, magical night they had spent together, until dawn had crept in over the rooftops of Paris.

But if the night had been for Nikos, then the day must only be for Ari—the reason they were here.

After lunch they went to the Luxembourg Gardens on the Left Bank, where Ari enjoyed himself at a children's playground and sandpit until it was time for an ice-cream while he watched the marionette theatre, hardly needing his uncle's translation of the traditional fairy tale depicted. After that came another ride on his beloved Metro, to a destination that left Ari speechless with glee—the descent into the sewers of Paris.

'I will explain everything to you while we are here, but it is not to be a subject for discussion over meals, Ari!' said his uncle sternly.

Nevertheless, the subject recurred, as Ann had known it would, over Ari's bathtime. He watched with a knowing eye as the water drained away, and explained its destination to her.

'Very good, Ari,' said Nikos from the doorway. 'And now I shall read your bedtime story while Auntie Annie makes herself even more beautiful than she always is.'

His eyes went to her, and their message was clear.

That evening they dined in the suite, with Ari fast asleep in Ann's room. They did not linger over their meal, superb as it was, washed down by vintage champagne. Instead, Nikos suffered her to swiftly check on Ari, before taking her to bed. And there in his arms she found a bliss that was unimaginable, sweeter, more wonderful, more thrilling than even the night before.

Afterwards, lying in the cradle of his arms, she wondered anew at the insanity of what she was committing, but she knew it was too late, and she was too helpless to resist. She shut her eyes to everything but the moment, content only to feel Nikos' strong arms enfolding her, to feel the beat of his heart beneath her cheek, the scent and taste of his body in her mouth as sleep washed over her.

But that sleep was rudely disturbed when more than the morning's sunlight pierced her slumber. Ari, waking to every expectation of another fun-filled day, had come to find her.

He bounced vigorously on the bed. 'Time to get up! Time to get up!' he enthused, landing with a thump.

As Ann stirred, and Nikos too, she saw Ari regarding them with keen interest.

'Mummies and daddies sleep in the same bed,' he pronounced.

'Well, so do uncles and aunties sometimes,' responded Nikos, sitting up, stretching his fantastic physique and looking not a whit abashed at being so discovered.

'Where are we going today?' asked Ari, accepting his uncle's comment without demur.

'A surprise,' said Nikos promptly.

He would not be drawn, despite his nephew's constant plaguing, but after breakfast a car was waiting for them, and it drove them out of Paris.

The surprise was another theme park.

'You're a glutton for punishment,' murmured Ann to Nikos, as they set off round the park for a day of rides and children's treats.

'But I have my reward waiting for me,' he replied, his dark

eyes glinting, and Ann felt heat flush through her skin. But even as it did she saw his expression change, become almost thoughtful for a moment, as if something had struck him.

She saw that look again during the day, from time to time, and sometimes, despite Ari's unbridled glee, Nikos seemed abstracted—his mind elsewhere. Perhaps he was thinking about work? thought Ann. Because surely he must be keen to get back to Athens?

She felt a pang go through her at the thought. Was this their last day together—tonight their last night? And what would come tomorrow? A car to the airport and Nikos and Ari heading back to Greece? Herself on a flight to London? To see Ari again—when?

And Nikos?

It was like a knife blade slipping into her. Silent. Deadly. And as it did so she felt the breath empty her lungs.

I can't bear to lose him!

She knew with every fibre of her being that there could never be another man like him in her life.

Knew as if a cold hand clutched her that for him she was just one more woman.

Yet it was so easy to forget that—dangerously easy. Not just when she clung to him in passion, or in the aftermath of passion, but during the day, when they were with Ari, together. As if—her heart squeezed—as if they were a family…

But they weren't—it was temporary, illusory, and that was all.

And yet the following day, when Nikos announced at breakfast that they were going to spend the weekend in Normandy, her spirits soared.

The elegant château hotel Nikos had booked was only a few miles from the coast, and their days were spent with Ari on the wide sandy beaches, and the nights entwined in the four-poster bed—with Ari, fast asleep from his exertions, in the connecting room.

It was over breakfast in their bedroom on the last morning that Nikos spoke to her. Ari was next door, watching cartoons on satellite TV.

'So, our little holiday is over and we must go home.'

Immediately Ann felt a chill numbness seize her. So this was the moment she had been dreading. The parting of the ways was upon her. She to return to London, Nikos and Ari to Greece. Even though she had known this moment must come, yet now it was here she felt as if a knife were sliding slowly into her.

Worse, far worse, than she had ever imagined it would be.

She felt the blood drumming in her head and fought for composure—outward at least, for inward was impossible. Yet even as she tried to control herself she became aware of what Nikos was saying next.

His eyes were resting on her with a strange expression in them. 'I want you to come back with us. Make your home on Sospiris.'

She could only stare, wordlessly.

His mouth twisted with wry self-mockery. 'Yes, you can stare, Ann. After everything I've thrown at you about *not* thinking you can insinuate yourself into our family. But obviously things are different now. Your making your home on Sospiris is the ideal answer. It ticks every box. You will be with Ari, and he with you. You get on excellently with my mother and Eupheme, and they both sing your praises—more than I have done!' he allowed, with the same wry expression. Then his expression changed. 'And best of all, Ann—' he picked up her hand and grazed the tips of her fingers sensuously with his lips '—we can still be together.'

His eyes were lambent, clear in their intent.

She waited for the leap in her spirits to come, for relief to flood through her at the blissful knowledge that she was not to be sent away after all, that Nikos still wanted her.

But it didn't come. Only a cold chill seeped through her skin. She heard herself speak, and hardly believed the words she was saying.

'I can't come back to Sospiris.'

She watched his expression change, as if everything were happening in slow motion.

'What are you saying?'

'I can't come back to Sospiris.' The brief words sounded so blunt, so harsh, but she said them again all the same.

His brows drew together, and he let go of her hand. In an instant he was not Nikos her lover, but Nikos Theakis to whom people did not say no...

Not even the woman he wanted to keep as an on-tap mistress in his home, spending her days with his nephew and her nights in his bed. A convenient mistress—there when he wanted her, while he wanted her. And when he no longer did—well, she'd still be looking after Ari.

She took a breath. A sharp one that cut like a knife. 'I have a life of my own. One I can't abandon indefinitely.'

His face had stilled. 'So this was nothing more than a passing amusement for you, was it?'

His voice cut as sharply as the breath in her lungs.

'There's nothing else it could be, Nikos. It's been a... a holiday. Wonderful, but—' another breath razored in her lungs '—now it's over.'

Even as she spoke her mind was shouting at her—urgently, desperately! *Don't say such things! Don't turn down what he is offering! Take it, grab it, seize it with both hands!*

But if she did—

The cold iced through her again. The icy cold of standing on the top of an Arctic crevasse. One wrong step and she would plunge down into its fatal depths. Her eyes went to him—went to the man who, night after night, had taken her into such bliss as she had never known, never could know again, whose arms had embraced her, whose kisses had melted her, whose smile alone warmed her like a living flame.

If I go back to Sospiris now—if I continue our affair—there can be only one ending, one fate for me.

A fate as clear to her here, now, as if it were already fulfilled. She said the words in her mind—forced herself to say them, to make very, very sure she faced up to them.

If I go back to Sospiris I will fall in love with him. Because already I stand on the brink of it—already I feel his power over me. But to him I will only ever be one more woman out of many. And one day he will have no more interest in me...

'And what about Ari?' Nikos's voice, still cutting, still cold, sounded again. 'You're just going to walk away from him?'

She felt her heart squeeze. 'It's for the best. I won't be out of his life. I can visit—or perhaps we can meet up. Your mother has been most generous in assuring me I am welcome for another holiday.'

'And that's all? All you're prepared to do? Very well.'

Abruptly, he got to his feet, looking down at her a moment. His face was closed. Closed to her completely. The way it had been for so, so long, until this brief, precarious truce had formed between them and this even briefer affair.

'Then there is no more to be said,' he finished. For one last moment he looked down at her, and for a second so brief she knew she must have only imagined it she saw something in his eyes—something that shook her. Then it was gone. Shuttered and veiled and closed down.

'You can have the task of telling Ari,' he said curtly. 'Since I'll be the one to mop his tears at losing you.'

She said nothing. Her heart was heavy enough as it was. Inside her head the voice was still shouting—telling her it wasn't too late, that there was still time to say she'd been an idiot, that of *course* she would jump ten feet at the chance to live on Sospiris, to take of him anything and everything she could, while she could, and not count the cost—never count the cost—until the bill had to be paid...

But when it does, it will be agony. So go—go now—while you can—while you can escape. Escape a fate that will be unbearable—year after year of watching Ari grow and knowing that Nikos has left you far behind...

She couldn't face it. Not even to stop Ari's tears, which came, as Nikos had said they would, despite all she could say to comfort him.

'I'll come and see you again, poppet. You know I will. Ya-ya has said so. And when you go back home Tina will be back—she'll want to know all about your lovely, lovely holiday...'

'But I want *you,* too—as well as Tina!' wailed Ari disconsolately.

Parting from him at the airport tore her, and yet again the voice in her head shouted at her to change her mind, recant, to go with them back to Greece, not board a lonely flight to London. But she had to do it—she knew she had to do it.

The pain now is bad, but it is to save myself worse pain. So I have to clutch that sanity, that sense, and take the lesser pain now. Whatever it costs me. Before it's too late.

But even as her plane landed at Heathrow, she knew, with a crushing of her heart, that it was already far too late. She was not standing on the brink of the abyss. She had already fallen deep, deep, *deep* into its fatal heart.

'Uncle Nikki, when will Auntie Annie come back?'

Ari's plaintive question cut Nikos to the quick.

'Not for a while,' he answered. 'But,' he said, forcing his voice to lighten, 'I've got nice news for you, Ari. Tina is going to come back to look after you. She'll come across from Maxos every day in the launch. In the evenings Maria will put you to bed, and get you up in the morning, but all day you'll have Tina.'

'I want Auntie Annie too,' said Ari dolefully.

'Well, we can't have her.' Nikos's voice was short.

No, neither Ari nor he could have Ann any more.

The familiar reaction kicked again, as it had done every time since he'd returned to Sospiris and faced up to the fact that Ann wasn't there any more. The villa, despite the presence of Ari, his mother, her cousin and all the staff, felt deserted—echoingly empty.

He wanted Ann there. Badly. He wanted her in the villa, just being there. He wanted her and he could not have her—and the knowledge kicked in him like a stubborn mule.

Why? Why the hell had she not wanted to come back here? Why the hell had she not wanted to be with Ari? And why the hell had she not wanted to be with *him?* Emotion roiled in him, angry and resentful—and more than that, but he would not acknowledge it.

Why had she walked out on him? Why?

The question went round in his head, over and over again, as if there might be an answer. But there wasn't one. How could there be?

We were good together! Hell, we were more than good, we were—

But his thoughts broke off, as if hitting a wall. A wall he didn't want to think about. Instead his mind went back to brooding—resentful, unforgiving—at Ann Turner, who had come willingly, so willingly, to his bed, whose possession had filled him with a searing fulfilment the very memory of which kept him sleepless, and who had lain in his arms as if there was no other place she could ever be. Yet she had walked out on him. Just—gone.

As if what we had was nothing to her. Nothing.

His brow darkened.

Why? Why had she done it? His face hardened. She'd said she loved Ari, but she'd been prepared to abandon him in tears. What kind of love was that? None. Ari clearly meant nothing to her.

Nor do I.

He felt the knife thrust again in his side. He tried to yank it out. Why should he care? He didn't care.

But even as he scored the words in his mind he knew them for the lie they were. He wanted Ann. He wanted her now, here—with him, with Ari, in his home, his life.

And he didn't have her.

He went back to his resentful brooding, his face closed and dark.

Work was all he could do, so he did it.

After five days on Sospiris—knowing he was being like a bear with a sore head, and knowing that the fact that his mother had received his curtly uttered intelligence that Ann had returned to London with nothing more than a placid calm only, illogically, made his mood worsen—he decided to take himself off to Athens.

His mother was just as placid and calm about his removal as she had been about Ann's desertion. And it aggravated him just as much. At the doorway of the salon he turned abruptly.

'I asked Ann to come and live here, to make her home here,' he said, out of the blue. He paused. 'She said no.'

His mother's eyebrows rose. 'Did she?'

'I thought she'd snap at it. Devoted to Ari as she is.' His brow darkened. 'As she claimed to be.'

'Well, she has her own life to lead,' Sophia Theakis replied tranquilly.

'She could have led it here,' her son retorted brusquely. 'And I could have—' He broke off.

'Perhaps,' his mother said gently, 'you didn't make your… request…sound sufficiently inviting?'

Nikos glowered at her. 'I told her it was the ideal solution. Ideal for her, and for Ari, and for m—' He broke off yet again.

His mother folded her hands into her lap. 'Nikos, my darling.' Her voice was different now. 'It's not something to undertake lightly. You must understand that. If Ann makes her home with us, here, not only does she have to give up her own life, but she has to think very carefully about what her life will be like here. We are not talking about a brief holiday—we are talking about years. Because the longer she is here, the more Ari would feel her loss if she were to leave again.'

'She doesn't have to leave again! She can just live here,' Nikos said stubbornly.

His mother looked at him. 'As what, Nikos? My permanent house guest?'

'No. As my—' He broke off.

For one long moment mother and son looked at each other. Then, his mouth pressed tightly, he spoke. 'I know what I want of her,' he said.

She looked at him measuringly. 'Do you?'

'Yes. And it is *not* the assumption you are making!'

The ghost of a smile played at Sophia Theakis's lips. 'But perhaps, my darling, I am not the only one making such assumptions?'

His brow furrowed. 'I don't understand what you mean,' he replied shortly.

His mother gave a gentle sigh. 'Think about it, my darling boy, on your way to Athens. Now, off you go—I'm sure you are keeping your pilot waiting.'

He took his leave, brow still furrowed. What did his mother mean? That *he* was making assumptions? Assumptions that Ann would want to be with him as much as he wanted to be with her? Angry resentment bit again. That was exactly the assumption he'd made. Of course he had! He'd had every reason to assume she shared his feelings!

Because why wouldn't she? He'd come to terms—belatedly, but finally—with the bitter circumstances surrounding Ari's birth. And if he could not exonerate Carla Turner's exploitation of Andreas, at least he could now pity her for what she had endured for her sister's sake. As for Ann, he'd come to terms, too, with why she'd taken his money—and why he'd hated her for the power she'd had to deny him his brother's child, then gone on hating her because he'd realised, when she'd come to Sospiris, that he desired the woman he had told himself he could only despise.

But that was all in the past! He no longer needed to despise Ann—now he could desire her to his heart's content. His face darkened again. Except she did not want his desire any more. She'd had enough. Taken what she'd wanted of him, enjoyed him, and gone.

Why? That was the question, stark and unanswerable, that went round and round in his head, as remorseless as the pounding blades of the helicopter taking him back to Athens. *Why?*

But it wasn't until that evening—sitting at his desk in his apartment, catching up with his personal finances for something to occupy a mind that wanted only to brood on Ann Turner's defection—that he got the answer to his question. And when he did, his fury with her knew no bounds.

CHAPTER FOURTEEN

IT WAS RAINING. Ann stared out of the window at the heavy skies and the soaking rain coming down in rods. She should go and finish her packing, ready to leave London. She felt her heart clench. What would she give to be heading back to Sospiris? No, she mustn't let her mind go there. Not in memory or in imagination or in anything at all. Nothing—nothing to do with anything about Sospiris, anything about Ari, and nothing at all, not an iota or a speck or a single mote, about Nikos Theakis.

But it was hopeless—hopeless to tell herself that. She had no power to ban him from her mind any more than she'd had the power to resist him when he'd wanted her for his bed. The only strength she'd found was in leaving him, and that had taken all she had. But it had been in vain.

The hammering at the door—demanding and peremptory—made her start. She got to her feet, making her way out of the room and along the narrow corridor to the front door—opening it.

Nikos Theakis was there.

Just as he had four long years ago he strode in, not waiting for an invitation. Ann could only stare, her heart pounding wildly, the blood leaping in her veins, her senses overcome with shock—with far more than shock. She hurried after him into the living room. Why, why was he here? What did it mean?

Hope—wild, insane—pierced her...

And crashed and burned. He turned, eyes blazing. But not with desire. Not with the emotion she had for a brief, fragile moment so desperately hoped for. Instead, with an emotion she had once been only too familiar with.

Loathing. Rage. Contempt.

Words seared from his mouth, twisted in fury, and his eyes darkened with blackest anger.

'You despicable little bitch!'

Her breath caught audibly. Then her face contorted. *'What?'* she demanded. Shock was slamming through her.

'What?' he echoed. 'You dare—*dare*—to stand there and plead ignorance? Did you think I wouldn't find out?'

'Find out what?' Shock was still numbing her. And something quite different from shock. Something that made her whole body, her whole being quiveringly, shakingly aware of the tall, dark figure that was dominating the space, taking it over. Her eyes were drawn helplessly, hopelessly, to his planed face, its features stark with fury. Even consumed with anger as he was, she could feel her senses leap at the sight of him.

'Don't stand there looking ignorant and virtuous! *Theos mou,* to think I was taken in by you. To think I found excuses for you. Justified your actions. *Forgave* you! And all along—'

Greek broke from him—ugly and harsh, withering her even though she understood not a word of it. He took two strides and was in front of her, hands curving over her shoulders like talons of steel.

'How dare you target my mother? Go sleazing to her with whatever disgusting tale you've trotted out?' His eyes were blazing—blazing with fury and an emotion that seared her to the spot. 'To think I wondered why you walked out on me in Paris. I wondered what could be so wonderful about your life without me that you could just dump me—abandon the child you prattled about loving. And now I know. *Now I know!*'

Breath razored from him. 'Did you think I wouldn't find out?' He gave a harsh, vicious laugh. 'Well, for your information I handle my mother's personal finances! Everything about her bank accounts goes through me. So tell me—' he shook her again, face black '—what lies did you spout to get her to part with so much money?'

Ann's eyes flashed fire. 'It was a *gift!* And I never, *never* asked for it! I didn't even know she'd given it until I got back here and found her cheque waiting for me in the post.'

'Which you cashed.' The words ground from him, enraged.

'Of course I cashed it. Just like I cashed the cheque you gave me to go out to Sospiris. And the cheque you gave me for taking Ari from me.'

'To fund your luxury lifestyle on other people's money!' His head twisted to take in the passport and travel documents on the table. 'And now you are fully funded to go off travelling again.' His hands dropped from her shoulders. 'So where is it to be this time? The Caribbean? The Maldives? The South Seas? What expensive destination are you heading for this time around?' Contempt dripped from his voice, lacing the anger beneath with savagery.

Ann's face set. 'South Africa,' she said.

'South Africa?' he echoed sneeringly. 'Isn't it the wrong time of year for there? Save it for the European winter—the Cape is very clement in December.'

'I'm not going to the Cape. I'm going inland. Up-country.'

'Ah—a safari!' His voice was withering her.

'No. I'm going back to work.'

His eyes flashed like dark lightning. '*Work?* You wouldn't know the meaning of the word. What kind of "work" do you intend to tell me that you do?'

'I teach. I train teachers. And I look after children.'

Derision etched his face. 'As if I would believe that! With all the money you've extracted from my gullible mother you can live a life of ease for the next two years at least!'

She shut her eyes. She'd had enough. Snapping open her eyes again, she shot back at him. '*That money was not for me.* Nor was the money you handed me to go to Sospiris—*nor* the money you gave me four years ago! I gave it away—all of it. To charity.'

He stilled. Then, as she watched him, feeling her heart pumping in her chest, a laugh broke from him. She could only stare. It was a harsh, mocking laugh.

'To charity? *Theos*, how you trot out your lies. Ann—' his eyes skewered her '—no one, *no one,* gives away that kind of money. No one gives a million pounds to charity when they're living in a squalid dump.'

Her mouth thinned to a white line. Wordlessly, she yanked out a folder from under her travel documents, thrusting it at him.

'Read that—*read it!* And don't you *dare* tell me what I did or didn't do with all that money!'

He took it, the sneer still on his face, the savage anger still in his eyes. But as he opened the folder, stared at the contents, she saw them drain away, leaving his face blank, his expression empty. He stared down at what she had thrust at him. Stared at the colourful leaflet lying on top of the other papers. He said something in Greek. She didn't know what it was, but she could hear the tone. Disbelieving. More than that. Shocked.

His eyes lifted. Stared at her. There was nothing in them. Then, as if every word were costing him, he spoke.

'You built an orphanage with the money?'

'Yes.'

The tips of his fingers were on the printed leaflet, which showed rows of dark, smiling children outside two substantial buildings, with a smaller one in between and one further on a little way away, all set amongst trees in a garden, with the hot

African sun beating down and a white picket fence all around. Around the entrance to each of the two larger buildings was lettering in bright colours. His finger traced the lettering.

'Andreas' House. Carla's House.' There was no expression in his voice, none, as he read out the names.

Nor in hers as she answered, 'One house for the boys, one for the girls. And a schoolhouse in between. The other building is a clinic, because so many of the children there are AIDS orphans and carry HIV. They need medicine and treatment. It serves the local community as well. The money you gave stretched to all of that.' She swallowed. 'It's where I went after I'd given up Ari. The charity I work for has more orphanages across southern Africa. There are so many children in need of care. The money your mother has so generously given can build another one, and run it too. She's been wonderfully, wonderfully kind—'

Her voice broke off. Nikos' eyes were resting on her.

'You told her? About the charity? Your involvement?'

Ann bit her lip. 'She asked me what I did and I told her. Why shouldn't I have? But I never asked her for money, Nikos! I told you—I didn't even know about this money until I got back to London. She wrote such a kind letter with the cheque—as kind as the one she wrote persuading me to give Ari up to her.'

'I thought my money had persuaded you.' There was something odd about his voice.

She shook her head. 'If I hadn't known—because of your mother's letter—how much Ari would be loved, cherished, how desperately she hoped he would help assuage the grief of losing your brother, I would never have willingly let go of Ari! But I was already working for the charity at its London office before Carla arrived, pregnant, and I was planning on going to work out in Africa anyway. Giving up Ari to your mother, giving your money to the charity, all seemed to fit together. And it helped me too—seeing those children there, orphans like Ari, but with no one to look after them. It…comforted me.'

She met his eyes, but they were veiled, shuttered.

'You told my mother—why didn't you tell me?' Again, there was something odd about his voice.

She gave a sigh. 'You didn't ask, Nikos. And you'd been so foul to me, I didn't see why I should try and justify myself to you. It's just as well, isn't it?' She looked at him with the faintest trace of bitterness in her eyes. 'You'd have just said I was lying to you…'

His mouth tightened, but not with anger.

'In Paris you could have told me. When I told you I understood why you'd been so tempted to take the money.'

'I was going to. But—' she looked away and swallowed '—I got distracted.'

'Not sufficiently distracted to stay with me when I asked you to.' There was more than tightness in his voice. Then, abruptly, it changed. 'But I had no right to ask you to stay with me. I can see that now. And I can see—'

His voice broke off. A deep, ragged breath was inhaled. His eyes went down to the leaflet in his hand.

'Andreas' House, Carla's House,' he intoned again, his voice stranger than ever.

'I asked for the houses to be called after your brother and my sister in their memory,' said Ann quietly.

His eyes lifted again, going to hers, and in them was an emotion she had never seen before.

'I thought so ill of you for so long,' he said slowly, as if the words were being prised from him. 'And you have shamed me, Ann. Shamed me as I have never felt shame before.' His face was heavy, stark. 'I came here full of self-righteous rage at you, and now—' He broke off again. His eyes went as if of their own accord to her passport. 'When do you go back to Africa?' His voice was blank, very neutral.

She answered in the same tone. All she could manage, despite the tumult raging through her. Not because she had finally told Nikos where his money had gone, but because…because seeing him standing there, so close and yet an impossible, unbridgeable distance from her, was agony. Agony….

'Tomorrow. I'd only come home on leave when I…when I saw you in that toy store. The charity was very understanding when I requested an extension to go to Sospiris. Besides—' she took a breath '—they were getting a huge donation in exchange. Worth a lot more to them than a few weeks of my time!' Her expression deepened. 'It's not so much extra helpers they need as funding. There's a never-ending need—the situation is so bad in so many parts of the region, even in the countries that are politically stable, let alone those with civil war or repressive governments. We do what we can, take in as many children as we can, but there are always more. Some are injured from landmines, and of course as well as AIDS there are other terrible tropical diseases afflicting them, so…'

She was rambling, she knew, but she was driven to talk. Driven to do anything other than face the fact that Nikos was here, in front of her, a hand's breadth away from her. All she'd have to do was just reach out to touch him, kiss him, go into his arms…

But she mustn't! She mustn't! He would be gone at any moment, all over again. Walking out of the door, away from her. Because what difference did it make, him knowing about her work. What she'd done with his precious money? Even if her pride and her anger at him had kept her silent, deliberately, knowingly, refusing to justify her acceptance of his money— because why should she care tuppence about being in Nikos Theakis' good graces after all the venom he'd spouted about her, about Carla? She'd let him call her names all the while knowing she could make him eat every one of them—and anyway having him look at her with such contempt had kept her safe from him, safe from doing what she had so, so wanted to do. What she had, in the end done despite all her best intentions and warnings.

She'd gone and done it anyway—fallen into his bed, and fallen in love with him… And it didn't matter, that her heart felt as if it were being sheared into pieces, torn up and minced and mangled and shredded, because nothing was going to change that—even if he did know now that she hadn't spent every last penny of his on herself, from luxury holidays to designer clothes, instead wearing Carla's—even if they were four years out of date, as Elena Constantis had spotted instantly, and even if they had only made Nikos think she'd spent his money on them.

Thoughts, emotions, words—all ran raggedly, crazily through her mind. And she let them run on because anything was a distraction from what was going to happen any moment now. Any moment now, Nikos was going to walk out of the door, and walk away…

Taking her heart with him…

And she couldn't bear it—she couldn't bear it. Not all over again. Seeing him again so briefly, so excruciatingly, and now he was going to go again. She would not see him for months and months, and when she did…when she did she would just be history—ancient history. An old flame, an ex—nothing more, nothing ever again…

She heard his voice, penetrating her numb anguish.

'Ann—'

She forced herself to herd her wild, desperate thoughts, forced herself to be what she must be now—calm, composed. Glad that he knew finally where his money had gone, that she wasn't the avaricious gold-digger he'd thought her after all. Glad that they could part without anger and contempt.

'Ann—' There seemed to be something strange about his face, his voice. Something almost…hesitant. But hesitation and Nikos Theakis were not words that went together.

But hesitant was, indeed, what his manner seemed to be. His eyes were still veiled, shuttered. Wary. There seemed to be tension visible in every line of his body.

'Ann,' he said again, 'once before I paid you for your time—insulting you grievously as I did so. But…but now that I know why you took my money, what your life actually is instead of my ugly assumptions, I…I wonder whether… whether you would consider…reconsider…your decision?' He took a deep breath. 'In Paris you said you had a life of your own to lead, and I respect that now entirely—indeed shamingly, for it shames me to think how you have dedicated your life to children who have so little. But if…if what you just said is true…that what is most valuable to those children is money, not western aid workers…then supposing I…I…gave enough money to…to make it unnecessary for you to go back, to hire someone in your place—?'

He stopped. Said something briefly, pungently in Greek, then reverted to English. 'I am saying this all wrong!' Frustration was in his voice. 'I am making it sound like I am trying to buy you out! But I don't mean it like that, Ann—I am simply trying to say that if my wealth would make it easier for you not to feel you had to go back to Africa yourself—if you could instead stay—come to Sospiris. To Ari.' He took another breath. 'To me.'

Suddenly out of nowhere his eyes were unveiled, unshuttered, a new expression blazing from them. She felt emotion leap in her—impossible to crush, impossible to deny. She couldn't move. She was rooted to the spot. Rooted as he stepped forward, took her face in his hands. And the touch of his fingers cradling her skull made her weak, and faint, and the closeness of his face, the heat of his gaze, the overpowering *thereness* of his body towering over her, so strong, so powerful, so *Nikos*…

'These days without you have been agony, Ann! I've been

impossible—impossible to live with! Angry and ill-tempered and short-fused and *hurting,* Ann—just hurting without you. Because I want you so much! I just want you back—back with me again. Because of what we had—what we've always had— even when I hated myself for wanting you, when I thought you were little better than your own sister, whom I thought then the lowest of the low. Even that could not stop me wanting you day and night. I was driven insane with not having you—until, thank God, my mother came up with her scheme for Ari's holiday in Paris. And then—even more thanks to God—I came to my senses over you and realised that you could not, *could not* be the person I had despised for four years. Having you respond to me was everything I'd been aching for, and I don't want to lose it. I want so much for you to come back to Sospiris with me now, and not go to Africa. Ari's missing you so much, and I...I am desperate for you, Ann!'

Her heart was cracking open. She could hear it. Feel, too, the agony in her muscles as she drew away from him.

'I can't, Nikos,' she whispered. 'I just can't.'

His hands dropped to his sides. 'Does your work mean so much to you?' There was emptiness in his voice.

She shut her eyes, her throat almost closing. Then she forced her eyes to open, to look at him.

'No,' she said. Then she said it. 'But you do.' She swallowed, never taking her eyes from his. 'You do, Nikos. And I know you didn't mean it—didn't even think about it. Because why should you? What we had in Paris was an affair—I knew that, knew that's all it could be. And that if I came back to Sospiris that was all it would be still. An affair. And one fine morning you'd decide you'd had enough of me, and the affair would be over. For you. But not—' her breath caught like a scalpel '—not for me. And I couldn't bear it, Nikos—living on Sospiris, helping to bring up Ari, and having to see you arrive with other women, see you choose, one day, one of them to be your wife, and knowing I was nothing more than yesterday's affair…'

He was looking at her. Looking at her with the strangest expression on his face. Words sounded in his head. His mother's voice. *But perhaps, my darling, I am not the only one making such assumptions.*

He'd thought she'd meant *him*. But she hadn't. Not in the least.

'*Theos mou,*' he breathed. 'You thought that? That I wanted you to come back to Sospiris because I wanted to continue an affair with you?'

Two flags of colour stained her cheeks. 'It's what you wanted before. When you offered me that diamond necklace. A clandestine affair in your mother's villa.'

A hand slashed violently, making her jump.

'God Almighty, Ann, that was then! When I still thought you as bad as I'd been painting you for four years! When my entire scheme was to slake my desire for you and remove you from my mother's house by seducing you! I was going to take you away from Sospiris—keep you as my mistress for as long as it took to make it impossible for my mother to invite you to Sospiris again! But how, *how,* after what we had in Paris, could you possibly think I only wanted an affair with you? I wanted—*want still,* desperately, with all my being—you to come back to me, to make a home for Ari, and for us to be *together.* You and me—a *family* for Ari and for us!' He took a hectic breath. 'It was hearing Ari's artless remark the morning he found us in bed together, saying that mummies and daddies slept together, that made it dawn on me that that was exactly what I wanted! For you and me to stay together.' He looked at her. 'To marry,' he said.

Shock was hollowing through her. Shock and other emotions even more powerful.

'To marry?' she echoed, as if she were uttering an alien language. 'Because then we could bring up Ari together?'

'Yes.'

'Because—' she swallowed '—we're good in bed together.'

'More than good, Ann,' he said dryly.

She dropped her eyes. She couldn't meet his, suddenly. Not without colour flaming in her cheeks at the way he was looking at her. And that wasn't what was needed—not now. Not now when she had to say the worst thing of all.

The hardest, cruellest thing.

'So a marriage for Ari, and for good sex?'

'Great sex,' he corrected her. 'And, of course, for one other reason.'

Slowly, as if they were weighted with lead, she made herself lift her eyes to him.

'What…what other reason?' Her voice was faint—as faint as she felt.

'Love, Ann,' he said.

She swayed. He caught her. Drew her to him. Not to kiss, but to hold, as lightly as swansdown. He smoothed her hair.

'Love, Ann,' he said again. 'I didn't know it until you left me. And now—now it's etched in stone upon my heart. Your name. For ever. And you love me, don't you, Ann? You said as much just now. So why not tell me, as I have told you?'

She shut her eyes and said it. 'I love you.' It was a breath of air, no more than that.

And then he folded her to him properly, wrapping his arms around her and she laid her head against his chest. At home. At rest.

'Nikos.' She breathed his name, resting against him. For a long, long while he simply held her. Then, easing back her head, he gazed down at her. Everything she could ever dream of was in his eyes.

And then in his lips.

EPILOGUE

IT WAS THE second wedding on Sospiris in as many months, and even more lavish than Tina's had been. She and Sam were both there, and this time it was Tina's turn to cry buckets—but she had come well prepared, as well prepared as Nikos's mother and Cousin Eupheme, with handkerchiefs to spare. Ari gazed bemused at them, and tugged his grandmother's sleeve.

'But it's a *happy* day, Ya-ya,' he explained to her. 'Auntie Annie's going to live here for ever and ever now. And sleep in Uncle Nikki's bed, just like in Paris. And I can wake them up—but not too early, Uncle Nikki says.'

Sophia Theakis laughed and stroked his head. Her cousin turned to her. 'It took them *such* a time, Sophia,' she sighed.

Nikos' mother nodded. 'The young are so blind, Eupheme. But it was obvious right from the first moment I saw them together that dear Ann, with not a mercenary bone in her body, would be ideal for Nikos. Spoilt by female adoration, he needed a good dose of animosity to challenge him. And, of course,' she added dryly, 'to be made to win her.'

'Oh, the sparks flew between the pair of them—they certainly flew.' Her cousin nodded.

'So much that they were blinding themselves to what was happening! When I saw them waltzing at Tina's wedding I thought they were seeing sense at last. But even that wasn't quite enough. I had to pack them off to Paris together.'

'Ah, Paris...' Eupheme sighed romantically.

'Indeed—and then the idiotic boy came back here alone. Goodness knows what he said or did to drive her away. But he obviously mismanaged the whole thing! So—' she sighed heavily '—I had to think of something else. It was as plain as day that Ann hadn't told him about the orphanage to commemorate my adored Andreas and Ari's poor dead mother, and I thought perhaps it was that that had come between them. It dawned on me that Nikki was bound to notice if I made a large donation myself, and it would send him back to her to find out why. Thank heavens it finally worked!'

'Yes,' said her cousin dryly, 'or you'd have had to develop a sudden urge to visit South Africa, Sophia...'

'I'm sure they have some very good cardiologists there,' replied Nikos's mother, even more dryly. 'And the climate would be excellent for my health too...'

They laughed together, and then the music was swelling, and Nikos and Ann were walking down between the congregation. Her hand was being held so tightly she doubted there could be any blood left in her fingers—but what did she care for that when her whole heart was singing, her eyes shining like stars? She turned her head to look at Nikos, and he gazed down at her, love in his eyes.

'My most beautiful bride,' he said.

'My irresistible husband,' she answered.

He dropped a swift kiss upon her mouth. 'That's the right answer,' he told her. 'Never leave me, Ann, and I will love you for ever!'

She laughed up at him. 'Oh, well, then you've got me for life, Nikos Theakis!'

Long dark lashes swept over glinting eyes. 'That's the

right answer too,' he said. 'And you have me, my own love, for all our lives together—and beyond—into eternity itself.'

Her breath caught, she was breathless with happiness, and then they were stepping out into the sunshine, man and wife, and Ari was running up to them.

Nikos scooped him up with a hug.

'Uncle Nikki.' Ari beamed, then turned to hold out his arms to his uncle's bride. 'Auntie Annie,' he said. She bent to kiss him heartily. 'And me,' he said. Satisfaction was in his voice.

'Family,' said Nikos.

And they were.

HARLEQUIN Presents

International Billionaires

Life is a game of power and pleasure.
And these men play to win!

THE FRENCH TYCOON'S PREGNANT MISTRESS
by *Abby Green*

As mistress to French tycoon Pascal Lévêque,
innocent Alana learns just how much pleasure can
be had in the bedroom. But now she's pregnant,
and Pascal vows he'll take her up the aisle!

Book #2814

Available April 2009

Eight volumes in all to collect!

www.eHarlequin.com   HP12814

HARLEQUIN® *Presents*

The LEOPARDI BROTHERS

*Sicilian by name…scandalous,
scorching and seductive by nature!*

CAPTIVE AT THE SICILIAN BILLIONAIRE'S COMMAND
by **Penny Jordan**

Three darkly handsome Leopardi men must hunt down
their missing heir. It is their duty—as Sicilians, as sons,
as brothers! The scandal and seduction they will leave in
their wake is just the beginning….

Book #2811

Available April 2009

**Look out for the next two stories in this
fabulous new trilogy from Penny Jordan:**

THE SICILIAN BOSS'S MISTRESS in May
THE SICILIAN'S BABY BARGAIN in August

www.eHarlequin.com   HP12811

HARLEQUIN *Presents*

kept for his
Pleasure

She's his mistress on demand!

THE SECRET MISTRESS
ARRANGEMENT
by **Kimberly Lang**

When tycoon Matt Jacobs meets Ella MacKenzie,
he throws away the rule book and spends a week
in bed! And after seven days of Matt's lovemaking,
Ella's accepting a very indecent proposal....

Book #2818

Available April 2009

**Don't miss any books in
this exciting new miniseries
from Harlequin Presents!**

www.eHarlequin.com   HP12818

UNEXPECTED BABIES

One night, one pregnancy!

These four men may be from all over the world–
Italy, a Desert Kingdom, Britain and Argentina–
but there's one thing they all have in common….

When their mistresses fall pregnant after
one passionate night, an illegitimate heir is
unthinkable. The mothers-to-be will become
convenient wives!

**Look for all of the fabulous stories
available in April:**

Androletti's Mistress #49
by MELANIE MILBURNE

**The Desert King's
Pregnant Bride #50**
by ANNIE WEST

The Pregnancy Secret #51
by MAGGIE COX

The Vásquez Mistress #52
by SARAH MORGAN

www.eHarlequin.com

HPE0409

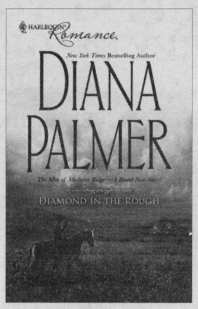

DIAMOND IN THE ROUGH

John Callister is a millionaire rancher, yet when he meets
lovely Sassy Peale and she thinks he's a cowboy, he goes along
with her misconception. He's had enough of gold diggers,
and this is a chance to be valued for himself, not his money.
But when Sassy finds out the truth, she feels John was merely
playing with her. John will have to convince her that he's truly
the man she fell in love with—a diamond in the rough.

THE MEN OF MEDICINE RIDGE—a brand-new miniseries
set in the wilds of Montana!

Available April 2009 wherever you buy books.

www.eHarlequin.com   HRI7577

REQUEST YOUR FREE BOOKS!

2 FREE NOVELS
PLUS 2
FREE GIFTS!

YES! Please send me 2 FREE Harlequin Presents® novels and my 2 FREE gifts (gifts are worth about $10). After receiving them, if I don't wish to receive any more books, I can return the shipping statement marked "cancel". If I don't cancel, I will receive 6 brand-new novels every month and be billed just $4.05 per book in the U.S. or $4.74 per book in Canada, plus 25¢ shipping and handling per book and applicable taxes, if any*. That's a savings of close to 15% off the cover price! I understand that accepting the 2 free books and gifts places me under no obligation to buy anything. I can always return a shipment and cancel at any time. Even if I never buy another book, the two free books and gifts are mine to keep forever.

106 HDN ERRW 306 HDN ERRL

Name	(PLEASE PRINT)	
Address		Apt. #
City	State/Prov.	Zip/Postal Code

Signature (if under 18, a parent or guardian must sign)

Mail to the **Harlequin Reader Service:**
IN U.S.A.: P.O. Box 1867, Buffalo, NY 14240-1867
IN CANADA: P.O. Box 609, Fort Erie, Ontario L2A 5X3

Not valid to current subscribers of Harlequin Presents books.

Want to try two free books from another line?
Call 1-800-873-8635 or visit www.morefreebooks.com.

* Terms and prices subject to change without notice. N.Y. residents add applicable sales tax. Canadian residents will be charged applicable provincial taxes and GST. Offer not valid in Quebec. This offer is limited to one order per household. All orders subject to approval. Credit or debit balances in a customer's account(s) may be offset by any other outstanding balance owed by or to the customer. Please allow 4 to 6 weeks for delivery. Offer available while quantities last.

Your Privacy: Harlequin Books is committed to protecting your privacy. Our Privacy Policy is available online at www.eHarlequin.com or upon request from the Reader Service. From time to time we make our lists of customers available to reputable third parties who may have a product or service of interest to you. If you would prefer we not share your name and address, please check here. ☐

HP08R

The Inside Romance newsletter has a NEW look for the new year!

Same great content, brand-new look!

The Inside Romance newsletter is a FREE quarterly newsletter highlighting our upcoming series releases and promotions!

Click on the Inside Romance link on the front page of **www.eHarlequin.com** or e-mail us at insideromance@harlequin.ca to sign up to receive your FREE newsletter today!

You can also subscribe by writing to us at: HARLEQUIN BOOKS Attention: Customer Service Department P.O. Box 9057, Buffalo, NY 14269-9057

Please allow 4-6 weeks for delivery of the first issue by mail.

IRNNEW09

You're invited to join our Tell Harlequin Reader Panel!

By joining our new reader panel you will:

- Receive Harlequin® books—they are FREE and yours to keep with no obligation to purchase anything!
- Participate in fun online surveys
- Exchange opinions and ideas with women just like you
- Have a say in our new book ideas and help us publish the best in women's fiction

In addition, you will have a chance to win great prizes and receive special gifts! See Web site for details. Some conditions apply. Space is limited.

To join, visit us at
www.TellHarlequin.com.

THBPA0108